INQUESTOR

Despatches from the High Inquest • Number Two •
October, 2018
Diplodocus Press • Bangkok • Los Angeles

Contents

An Introduction to *The Darkling Wind*   3
by Theodore Sturgeon

Message from the High Inquest   6
Taboos and Sexualities in the Disperal of Man

Poetry   11
by S.P. Somtow

The Homeworld of the Heart:
A Woman Cloaked in Shadow
by S. P. Somtow   13

Primer on the Inquestral High Speech - Part II
by Prof. Schnau-en-Jip   96

Lost Tales
The Dust   101
by S.P. Somtow

Interview 135
by Darrell Schweitzer

Despatches from Earth 149
Madama Butterfly in the Age of Human Trafficking
by S.P. Somtow

Notes From Beyond the Overcosm 154
Letters from our readers

The Inquestor Series 155
List of Titles

© 2018 by Somtow Sucharitkul. All rights to material not by Somtow Sucharitkul are the property of their creators.
ISBN: 978-1-940999-17-3

Diplodocus Press
Bangkok • Los Angeles
www.diplodocuspress.com

An Introduction to *The Darkling Wind*

by Theodore Sturgeon

What's that you have in your hands?
A book, you say.
No, it isn't.
A novel, then?
No — it's more than that. It began to be a novel three novels ago.
What, then? Some kind of explosion?
No; one can't even say that. (Don't be alarmed; it won't go off in your hands.) No; because there's one characteristic of all explosions; like plucked strings, they begin to decay the very microsecond they reach their peak. This book doesn't.
What is it then?
Ah. So many things. It is the fourth part of a trilogy. It's a shattering storm that whirls away, leaving your world full of brilliance and cacophonies of color — but never leaves its residence just over the horizon. It's an adventure — yours, perhaps much more than the adventures of its array of astonishing characters. It's (to use a critic's cliché) a mind-stretching experience; few if any writers have even attempted the description of a universe so vast, nor the almost limitless power — and powers — within it. Yet never for a moment is it out of the author's control, and therefore out of the reader's understanding (or at least, his

comprehension. There are things which simply *are* which passeth understanding; but this young giant never enters the intangible through laziness. Listen:

> There is a difference between the old gods and the new. The important thing is that the new gods are moulded in man's image. They do not seek to force mankind into something it is not: they are ideals, not entities. You have seen the consequences ... of having gods that actually exist! In freeing them, we have returned to them the right to fashion their own gods.

Throughout his work, Sucharitkul breaks the reader's pace (never his own!) with asides so provocative that one must, with great reluctance, guide oneself to the banks of his stream of narrative, and sit and think it out:

"Truth, my dear friend, is merely the prevailing percentage of our private illusions."

Take that before breakfast, my dear friend, and it will surely alter you day.
***

I have a confession to make: I don't make a habit of blowing deadlines, but I have done so drastically this time, and for a very interesting reason. A part of my confession is this: I have developed a curmudgeonish impatience with the current rash of trilogies, tetralogies, multi-volume 'epics', 'sagas' and so on (and on.) (Unless, of course, they're written by Marion Zimmer Bradley, Quinn Yarbro, or their rare ilk.) I've tried to be fair; as a reviewer, I hide behind the phrase "For those who enjoy ..." and keep the curmudgeon in check. But I heard Somtow read a portion of his *Vampire Junction* and was quite carried away, and produced a fulsome review for the Washington *Post*, which resulted in the request that I introduce this — this which you hold in your hands. Reading it, I wanted to know more (not that exactly; tater, I wanted to bathe more in this chiaroscuro of style and movement(and found

myself avidly and attentively reading this book's precursors: *Light on the Sound, The Throne of Madness,* and *Utopia Hunters.* One cannot read with such attention and intensity within the confines of short deadline-time; at least I couldn't and didn't. My gratitude, therefore, to your editor, Chris Edwards, for his monumental patience. The result of this long immersion in these four great books has been that I have not more to say to you, but less. My greatest wish is that the work speaks for itself to you, and not that I speak for you. I think that the best way to express it is to say that deeply envy anyone who has not read the tale of the Inquestors, for they have before them this transcendent experience.

***

A last word, concerning Somtow personally. Write as he does, at times, about murder-en-masse and buckets of blood, he is one of the gentlest, most well-mannered and engaging people I have ever encountered. He looks like a smiling teenage Buddha. He has been seen (at this writing, 1985) increasingly at conferences and conventions; if the occasion arises for you to be in his presence — be there.

I don't know what his age is.

Perhaps he doesn't have one.

— Theodore Sturgeon
Springfield, Oregon

Message from the High Inquest

Taboos and Sexualities in the Dispersal of Man

As of this writing, *Inquestor Tales No. 1* has been out for a short time. Over 70 people have taken the bait of getting a free kindle copy from Amazon (that's on the first day). Two people have actually purchased a physical copy. I have to admit it's a bit of a slow start, but yes, I've made around $6 off this novel now. Awesome!

As to how to parlay the six bux into the millions this saga undoubtedly deserves (in the mind of at least one impoverished writer) ... I thought it might be time to touch on some of the aspects in the series that are ... let us say ... *forbidden*.

The stories in the Inquestor series first appeared in *Analog* and in *Isaac Asimov's Science Fiction* magazine. The time was the 70s, and through the first half of the 80s. Emerging from the "free love" era, science fiction was still a little constrained, because most of its authors were still very white, very male, mostly straight, and somewhat suburban; diversities were only just emerging. Indeed, I was at one time pretty much the only Asian science fiction writer to penetrate this exclusive world, and the few women who were there were often quite ... unorthodox. They were known by the extraordinary sobriquet of *femmefans*. When I entered the community, it was still very much a male-dominated one, and the great science fiction of the Golden Age which preceded my advent was also male dominated. For a long time after I entered the field, many of the most powerful works had few women in them, or had women who existed only to serve tea to the important scientists who were often the protagonists.

Writing mostly in *Asimov's* which at the time was a bit retro in some ways, one didn't really break too many sexual taboos, but the novels began to sneak away from this.

I was on a panel with, among others, David Gerrold, well known writer of the *Star Trek* episode "The Trouble with Tribbles" and I casually mentioned a brief scene in *The Throne of Madness* "where two boys make love in a desert of powdered chocolate."

To my surprise, David became very interested in this and demanded to know the page number. I suddenly realized that despite science fiction's staid reputation, it was actually one of the only genres in which one could explore things that were not talked about in whitebread American society. I was rather embarrassed to tell him that the entire sex scene was over in a single sentence.

Books and stories that really blasted holes in these taboos were often written by women — I'm thinking of Ursula le Guin's *The Left Hand of Darkness* or Joanna Russ's *When It Changed*. I'll never forget that in one of Vonda McIntyre's future civilizations, asking a stranger "Is there anything I can do?" meaning "Do you want sex?" was a matter of normal politeness, and refusing anyone of any gender was viewed as a bit rude.

As the Inquestor series gradually left the magazines and grew into novels, I started to evolve a picture of the sexuality of that universe, which follows completely different assumptions from most modern cultures. The Inquestors themselves, rather like Imperial Romans, have no inhibitions. On most planets, servocorpses perform menial tasks and are also freely used for the satisfaction of any sexual urge however "perverted" — much as slaves were during the Roman period. But the fact that they are corpses, and presumably lacking in real feelings, gives this institutionalized necrophilia a kind of macabre justification.

It is fair then to say that in Inquestral societies, apart from extremely isolated worlds or worlds deliberately keeping themselves apart from mainstream culture, there really are no sexual taboos as such, especially when such acts are performed with corpses. Between humans, there is a hierachy of constraint; from no constraint at all for the highest, the Inquestors, down to a more hidebound sexuality for the lower orders (who are still permitted anything they want as long as it is with the dead.)

In *Homeworld of the Heart*, the Inquestor universe toys with autoeroticism of a kind that can't be found in our world — a powerful love for a manufactured clone of oneself — even though Sajit and Tijas are perhaps too immature to really understand these urges. They are really somewhat inchoate; whether the urges are finally acted upon is a matter that probably won't be answered in this book. Though I'm still writing it — who knows?

It's not only sexual mores that are different in this universe; the casual assumption that children are the only possible soldiers because they have the best reflexes, the implicit caste system dictated by clan-names (caste by Inquestral fiat rather than by birth), and the basic premise of Inquestral philosophy — that utopias must be eliminated because they will lead to stagnation.

Which brings us to a a widespread taboo on Urna and many nearby worlds, one that was found in Stone Age societies (even to this day) on earth, but which most civilized people find absurd — the taboo against twins and by extension dopplings. It seems as ridiculous as a taboo against left-handedness, but both taboos were once commonplace in early societies.

When interviewed by Darrell Schweitzer a very long time ago, I said that I wanted to create a universe of incredible beauty *and* brutality in the Inquestor series. One of the ways of doing this is to extrapolate from primitive earth societies, supposing that they had powerful future technologies. The amount of brutality possible increases exponentially.

Beauty is another matter. It is in the eye of the beholder.

Please let me encourage you to write letters of comment, as this is a personalzine in format, even though it is more high-tech than in the heyday of fanzines.

The easiest way is for you to write a note to *inquestortales@bangkokopera.com,* an email address created just for this perhaps. I'll publish the most entertaining or thought-provoking ones.

— Somtow

On Seeing a Cigarette Butt in the Butt of a Stone Lion in Angkor Wat

a sonnet

One sun-drenched, sweltering day in the Khmer
High tourist season, I sought shade behind
A headless beast. A pool of moisture where
Some Philistine had taken time to grind
A cigarette butt into ancient stone.
I had an Ozymandias moment, hearing
The past, shrieking through fields of bone,
And into vacuous sunlight disappearing.
Faceless it was today, but once that fierce
Leonine countenance struck starkest terror;
Once there were eyes whose irate gaze could pierce
Men's souls, and chastise every mortal error.
In Jayavarman's dreams this lion roared
Now it's a butt joke for a tourist horde.

— S.P. Somtow

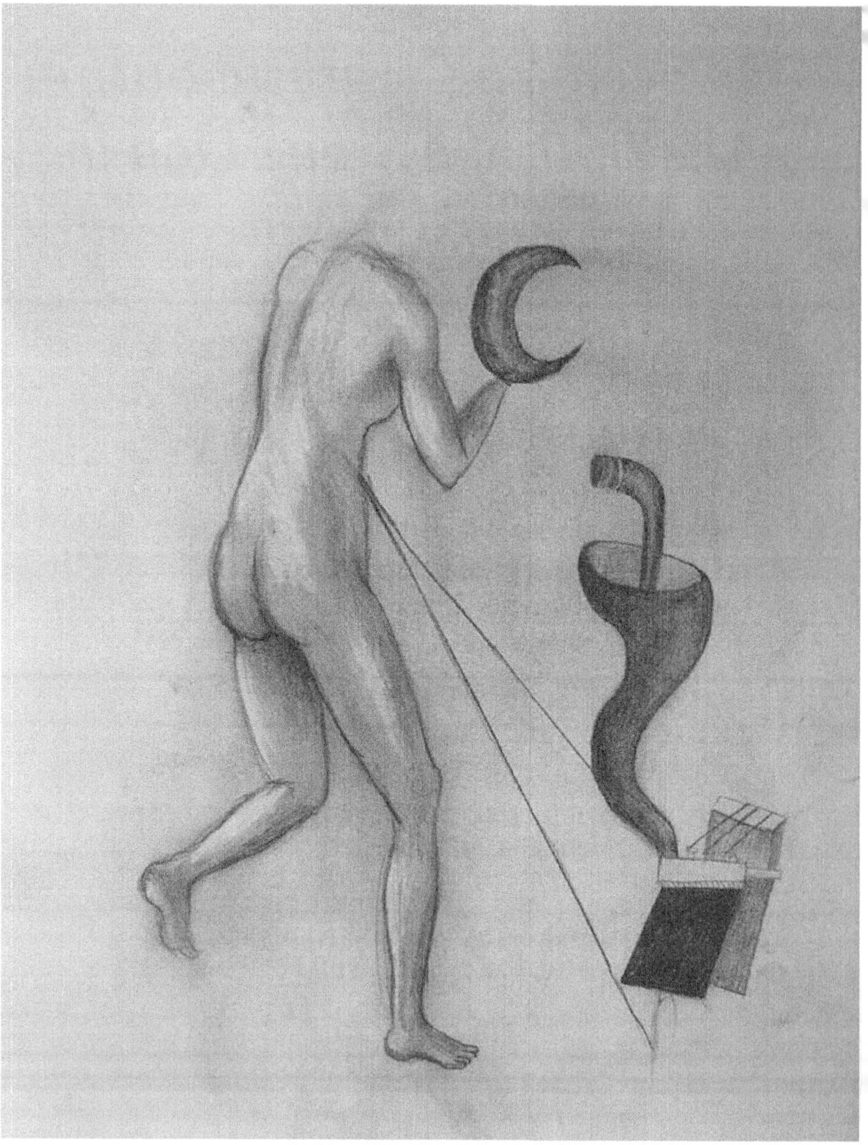

CHRONICLES OF THE HIGH INQUEST
The Homeworld of the Heart

by S.P. Somtow

Book Two
A WOMAN CLOAKED IN SHADOW

din veó qatávuten
z' rashkhítonens ombrá
din veó qatávuten
a vórtuen et únisheh
moréh shiveléh telaveóreh
dashtéh vornekéh
den o-savezhut át ás
ma din meáh sazhío

*I saw you framed
in a shimmercloak's shadow
I saw you framed
by the gateway to nowhere*

*mother, sister, prophetess,
goddess, whore,
what you were I knew not
but I knew you were mine.*

— from *The Songs of Sajit*

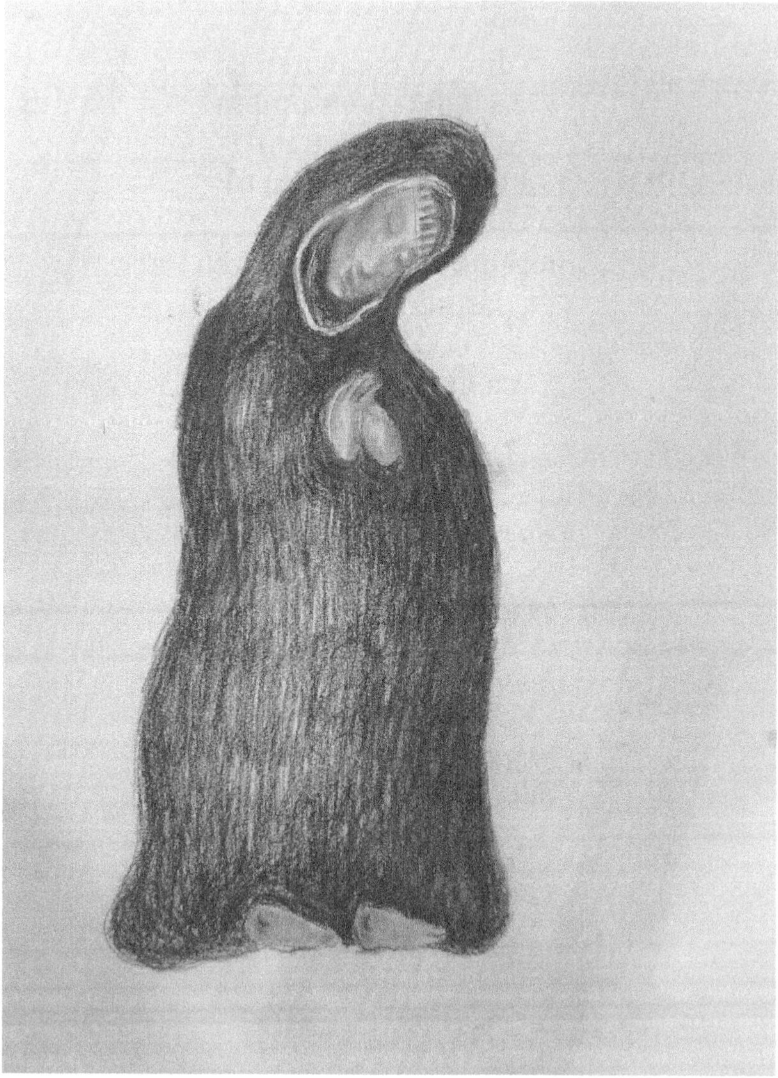

Five
Cloaked in Shadow

The Rememberer continued:

In fact, she was no supernatural vision, though to the febrile imagination of a unformed bard she may have seemed so. She was a woman. She had a name.

Her name was Éluma, which in the highspeech means *soul*. She was a priestess of the mysteries of Aërat, that is to say a prostitute, for there had not been a cult of Aërat, or any other deity, in Urna, for at least a millennium; yet sometimes the ancient titles were useful euphemisms.

Éluma had been apprenticed to Aërat since the age of five; she had lived in the House of the Priestesses of Aërat, also called the House Without Walls, also called the Labyrinth of Shadows, in Shírensang in the shadow of Nevéqilas, studying the art of arousal, until the appropriate time when she would perform the rituals in the real world.

Not that practice was difficult. The temple had a large supply of highgrade pleasure corpses, calibrated according to size, number of appendages and openings, quality of appearance, level of cosmetic enhancement. One could do exercises with a soma of any type, whether a withered old lecher or an innocent first-timer, with responses programmed for randomness as well as for characterization. The art of Aërat required a different face for every client, a different voice, different technical accomplishments; a servant of the god could specialize, but some skills were common to all.

Éluma's specialty was in making the client feel loved. Passion she could do, games she could play, but love is the hardest of all the skills, the only one that cannot be faked.

Bequeathed to the temple as a child, Éluma grew up with only virtual knowledge of the world, as devotees did not were not allowed to leave until the day of their dedi-cation ritual. In the main, she had been raised by servocorpses. She did not have friends; contact with real human beings was not allowed, for fear that the acolyte might learn to *receive* passion, rather than *be-stowing* it.

Perhaps an entire tribe of Rememberers would be needed to catalog her childhood and her young womanhood, even though the world she lived in was not real.

Yet there were scenes that seemed real enough....

***

Éluma was free to wander the labyrinth that was the dwelling place of Aërat. Often she would be guided by one of the instructor servocorpses. Occasionally there would be another in-itiate, being hurried through a corridor, and sometimes their eyes would meet; that was the only way Éluma knew there were others here.

Servocorpses' eyes are not the eyes of the living.

Once a boy ran through the cross-corridor, a boy whose hair was a cold blue flame; they looked at each other and the girl's eyes were the color of the flame; and the boy said to her, "I don't know!" and she tried to smile, but soon Éluma was hustled down a side passage, and the servocorpse, not a talking model, covered his mouth so he could not answer.

When he was gone, Éluma said, "What is it he did not know?"

The servocorpse could not reply, but led her by the hand, quickly, and by a circuitous route Éluma found herself once more in an instruction chamber.

***

There was a room called the Hall of the Goddesses. There, one could study every image of Aërat since the foundation of the temple. There were statues in stone and holosculptures and plas-tiflesh. There were automata and tapestries.

On one occasion she found herself there, not knowing which pathway she had taken. When she entered, there was something — a servocorpse — swabbing at a monu-mental sculpture with a depulverant. The corpse skittered away when it saw her. The room was gloomy, though it was well lit; it was dusty, though there was no dust. Each of the subjects seemed to cast an aura. Row upon row, each bearing the same face, the face that many believed was perfection itself, the face of Aërat.

That was where she saw I-don't-know again. He was bent over a stand on which stood three miniatures of the Goddess, carved in phoenix ivory; they had set in a miniature rock garden, and had portrayed the three sacred gestures of the Goddess — *Come Hither, I Shall Love You Forever,* and *Destiny is our Destiny.*

"They must very old," Éluma whispered.

"A few minutes, at least," the boy said. His hair moved as though on an artificial wind. It was, she realized, some kind of symbiont, not a flame at all.

"But the age of phoenixes was five centuries ago," she said, proud of her history.

"Idiot! I'm not looking at any damn statues." He pointed at the miniature rock garden and Éluma saw them now: tiny blue filaments, like the ones on the boy's head, wriggling between the white pebbles.

The boy yanked out a strand of his hair and dropped it onto the rock garden.

"Does that hurt?"

"Only if I let it."

"What do they live on? Don't they need an organism to feed them, not just a bunch of white pebbles?"

"You really are an idiot, little whore."

"I'm not —"

"We all are. In training at least. Now look at the stones. Look for a long time. Why does this little stand have a metal bevel? Why would pebbles want to run away?" What do they flee from?"

When Éluma looked again, when she really stared, she could see that the pebbles were not entirely still. Rather, each was expanding and contracting, as though they were breathing.

And the statues ... they two were not motionless. For each one's joints were slowly ... every few seconds ... shifting. Each gesture was slowly transforming into the next gesture. This static tableau was in fact a thing of constant movement, if one had but the patience to more than just glance at it.

"I won't ask your name, because here we have no names," the boy said. "But remember the lesson. Nothing holds still forever. Oh! Got to run."

The boy looked furtively around and then — to Éluma's astonishment — an arm popped out of the empty space behind him, seized him by the edge of his tunic, and pulled him into nothingness.

"Fooled you! I'm still here!" A voice, ringing in the nothingness.

She never found that room again.

***

There was a room they called *The Clouds and Rain*. In this room, there were no horizons. You floated, but you were not weightless. You were surrounded by cushiony, velvety nothingness. The air had texture. You could twist your body into any position and the air would hold you; the air was as viscous and as vacuous as it needed to me, bending itself to every movement; it was said that the air was made of the same creature that formed the shim-mercloak, a single celled organism that enveloped an entire Inquestor, trans-forming his inner light into a pale twilight glow.

A dream lover dwelt in this room.

You enter the room via a mirror that is really a displacement plate. You are in your room, little more than a cubicle because you have no possessions: your entire life is for giving, never for receiving; your duty is to be-come the desired.

You look at yourself in that mirror, and as you have been trained, allow each thought to drain from your mind, down a sinkhole of forgetfulness; a circle of blackness deepens, widens, until you feel yourself dissolving into the image of yourself in the mirror....

... and when you hit that moment of total inner darkness can the displacement be triggered ... and you find yourself inside the room....

... and the lover comes.

The lover is invisible. Genderless, it seems ... but not an *it*, either; rather the lover is all genders and all varieties of lovemaking. The lover embraces, suffuses the air, penetrates every opening, every pore. The lover envelops. The lover overwhelms. The lover batters down the battens of your soul, bares open your heart; you lose yourself in the lover, you pour yourself into the lover, the lover, the hungry vessel, the lover who takes and takes though you never stop giving ...

... and when you are spent, the darkness swoops down and you awaken in the room that it is little more than a cubicle. And the clouds and the rain cling to your flesh are can never be wiped away.

That is the nature of your art.

You are the mirror of your lover's soul; your very being is to give. There is no self. There is only the lover.

More than that, there is only technique; the flick of the finger, the seven categories of caress, the basic movements of tongue and hips and hands and lips; all these catalogued and endlessly to be recited, analyzed, and reinvented.

***

She wondered if she would ever see *I-don't-know* again. In the refectory, perhaps, she might catch a glimpse. Or during one of the big instruction halls, where each person was alone, cocooned in a bubble of force, but one could sometimes catch another person's eye.

What was today's lesson going to be.

Today's lesson was about touch.

Then why aren't I allowed to touch anyone? What is so special about dead people?

***

In the room, Éluma knew she was alone, though around her there were other acolytes. The others could be seen from the corner of the eye, sometimes, vague flitting shapes; Éluma imagined that for each of the other novices she too was a vague shape, sometimes a shadow, sometimes a gust of breath. The instructor was a holosculpt of the goddess herself; the demonstrator was a servocorpse, so androgynously retooled that one could see in it any gender one wished to see.

Today's demonstration, said the voice of the goddess, *is about levels of moisture in the tongue, and how to control them. Between dry and wet there are seven progressions, com-*

parable to the shrut of a musical scale....

Éluma tried to concentrate. But her mind went back to the secret room behind the mirror, to the secret lover ... and she longed to receive instead of give, to be an object of love rather than a repository of love. She let the words of the goddess swirl about her ears while her mind repeated again and again *Love me for who I am.* A heretical thought, but one that was keeping her sane, feeding her a figment of hope.

Slowly move your tongue across the edge of your lower lip ... not too fast ... Éluma, your mind is drifting!

"Oh ... sorry, Goddess."

You are not, Éllekeh. You are rarely sorry. It's one of your most endearing characteristics. Do not fear. The time of your unbinding is soon to come.

"Unbinding, Goddess?"

"You've had your womanblood. Your mastery of my arts is among the highest among my acolytes. I must warn you now, child, that you will not know when your test will come; you will know only when you have been awarded the cloak of shadow."

So Éluma came to know that sometime, in the near future, her status would change; that it would come without warning; and that there would come a time when she would emerge from the cocoon of the temple, and live no more among the dead. She did not know if this pleased her, because she barely remembered the living; she had been pledged to the temple very young.

To pay a debt, perhaps, or to fulfill a vow.

***

Only in the refectory could one ever really talk to other acolytes; meals were shared, each table seating two, in order to further instruct in the art of conversation. Conversations were, of course, rehearsed, from preexisting scripts.

One morning, indeed, she saw the boy again, the boy she thought of as "I-don't-know." They were assigned as dialogue-partners. He was good enough at the pleasantries, pouring the *zul* and passing the honeyed salt with the right bend of the wrist, but he stumbled when it came to conversation itself.

"The weather been cloudy," she said to him, because that was one of the standard dialogues they had to memorize. The correct response would have been, "But not so cloudy as when we make the rain." The art was always to turn the subject towards the sensual.

Instead, he grasped both her hands. "My name is Mikkálu, called Mikeh," he said. Names are never exchanged in the temple of Aërat. The servocorpse who doubled as a waiter jabbed the boy with an electroflagellum; politely, Éluma ignored what was one of the petty indignities of being an acolyte, the fact that dead people were allowed to punish you.

"No, no, I want someone to know my name."

The servocorpse made another move, but Mikeh grabbed the flagellum from its hand and lashed it in the face. He had pushed up the setting; it actually lacerated the dead one's cheek, and a phlegmatic pseudo-blood oozed from the wound.

"Yes, I'm aggressive," Mikeh said. "I'm not able to lose myself in someone else. That's why they're not even letting me take the test."

"Test?" Éluma remembered that the Goddess had told her a test was coming soon.

"I wanted someone to know my name before they send me away."

"Away?" That was strange to Éluma, who after all knew only these halls, these corridors and pathways.

"I'll be a childsoldier," said the boy. "Remember my face. One day you'll see me riding the clouds, but there won't by any phantom lover with me. You'll look into my eyes and you'll see death."

They led him away.

***

The test that Éluma faced a few sleeps later could not have been more strange. She was led into an empty room, in the middle of which there was a completely circular bed. A man sat on that bed and she gasped.

"I didn't know they had a servocorpse made to look like —" Without even think-ing, she had started to pro-strate herself. Every Princeling in Urna would appeat identical to every other; they were the only family in the world accorded the privilege of doppling. Abhorrent and abominated though it was to divide one flesh again and again, doppling the prince-ling gave the culture of this world continuity and fulfilled the great Inquestral adage: *History there is, and no history.*

And there was the image in the flesh. Not old, not young, with a simple grey kilt held in place by a living serpent.

A triumph of the the art of servocorpse manufacture! "Am I real to you?" Yes; it was a voice she had heard in the air around her, in a holo-broadcast, declaiming at her from the pages of a book.

She could barely answer. "It resembles the High Princeling Orifec in every regard," she said, addressing the servocorpse in the third person as befit its devived condition.

"They say," said the simu-lacrum, "that this model verges on lèse majésté, and should never be shown in public. But never mind that; we're not in public now."

Overcome with the feelings that had been ingrained in her all her life, she did prostrate herself at last. "Starry Highness!" she murmured.

He whispered a word and the walls deopaqued and she found that they were surrounded by images of rain-bow-fringed clouds.

And then he touched her.

She did not know where her training ended and her feelings began. *I must not feel,* she told herself. *Do my duty. Be the empty vessel of the client's longing.* And yet, she tingled at the slightest graze. And she found herself saying, over and over, "Do you love me?" which were forbidden words, but she could not help herself.

I thank the goddess this is merely a test, she told herself. And their lovemaking continued, and it was as though she were back in the secret ocean of the room without horizons.

And when it was over, she lay on the embankment of cloud, created from holosculpture and imagination. She looked into his eyes and wondered if there was not a flicker of life in them. But that would not have been possible. Tired out, she slept, and when she woke she was again in her cubicle, just another acolyte of Aërat, just another prostitute in training.

***

It was a tennight later that they came for her. The corridors were new to her. Some doors were physical, some doors were displacement plates. She was march-ed in so many directions she lost all sense of space. And at length she reached a room she had never seen. It was a council chamber of sorts. There was an empty throne at one end; the intagliata of mating serpents was instantly recognizable. On either side sat a matronly figure; these appeared to be powerful administrators of the temple. And in front of the throne, standing, was the Goddess herself; not a holosculpt, but in the flesh, for she reached out tousled Éluma's hair, and there was a tear in the corner of one eye.

"Éllekeh," said the Goddess, calling her by her childname. "Today we will honour you with a cloak of shadow. You have been singled out, and you will soon be leaving this place. The temple has been like a womb to you, forming you in the image of the thing that all desire, that you may serve me, the eternal Goddess of Love. To serve Love, you have renounced Love; your life will be a perpetual giving, never receiving."

Behind the throne and on either side, shrouded in shadow, were other acolytes. All, it seemed, in the flesh. Most wore the shapeless covershawl that made them indistinguishable from one another. One of them was not so dressed.

It was, she realized, Mikeh, the boy whose hair was a cold blue flame; the boy was already wearing the simple tunic of a childsolder in training, and his eyes had become yellow; he was in the first stage of the im-plantation of the citrine-colored laser-irises that would render him into the most effective killing machine in the Dispersal of Man. It must have taken some doing to have let him attend the ceremony, but as Mikeh himself had said to her, "I'm aggressive." He was standing slightly apart from the others, and behind him there was a tall woman in some kind of offworld uniform.

She mouthed a greeting; he looked sullenly at her, but at least there was a real connection.

The Goddess said, "Before you receive your cloak of shadow, Éllekeh, there will be one final ritual: the Smoothening."

"Goddess, what is this? This was not in the instructions."

"No," said the goddess. "This ritual is secret. It is what binds you to us. From now on, you will be able only to give, and never to receive. Your body is a temple, but when you were born there were some rough edges, some small blights that stand in the way of pure perfection. The mental and emotional edges have been smoothened through years of training. This is the final stage. Your body, too, shall be made smooth and perfect. There will be no pain."

The two matrons approached. They pulled tools from their cloaks. Sharp, shiny tools.

"From now on, you can be all things to all clients. You can be any gender, any variety, any combination."

A third matron emerged now, holding a tray of prosthetics. "Whatever you need, you shall have them all," said the Goddess. "Whatever is called for; boy, girl, crone, maiden, youth, dotard, whatever the love object in the client's fantasy may be...."

Éluma screamed.

And the boy named Mikkálu, whose name was unknown to all but Éluma, sprang up and put himself between Éluma and the matrons who were now brandishing scalpels and shears. "They're lying to you!" he shouted. "They're going to cut out the roots of your feeling!"

"Be calm," said the Goddess. "We have done this for centuries here in the Temple of Aërat. It is a privilege, an honor. I assure you, my child, there will be no pain."

The first matron held up a knife high while servocorpses carefully held Éluma still and began to pry open the seam of her robe —

Mikkálu leapt.

He whirled in the air. A line of yellow light lanced the air. A smell of burning flesh —

The matron's arm, still clutching the knife, still wriggling as if alive, separated, lying on the white tiles of the council chamber.

The woman, in shock, did not even scream. The laser strike had cauterized and sealed the stump and the arm. "I can kill you all," Mikeh said.

Then came a cold blue glow from the empty throne. A figure slowly formed, first in outline, then the shape slowly filling in; the bright-eyed one, not old, not young, wearing the simple kilt. Éluma freed herself from the servocorpses' grip.

"You were real!" she gasped.

Around her, everyone had fallen to the ground in prostration. But she could not do it. Not after what had happened between them.

"I am," said the man, "the Son of the Starlight, the High Princeling Orifec z'Urnasi Tath, hereditary Lord of Nevéqilas, Commander of the World Entire, He Who Answers Only to the High Inquest. "

Even the Goddess was on her knees, and Éluma saw with some bitterness that she was no goddess; she was merely an actress, playing a role in a drama that had been enacted in this temple for generations, born not from logic but from caprice, or superstition. And so she still found she could not prostrate herself.

"Take the wounded woman away and give her another arm," he said. Some servocorpses obeyed. "Now, childsolder, speak to me."

"I am Mikkálu-without-a-Clan," the boy said. "I was sold to this place when I was seven. A gambling debt."

Orifec laughed a little. "That explains your ... recalcitrance," he said. "They didn't get you early enough. How did you manage to be accepted as a childsoldier?"

"I was disobedient too often, Starry Highness. They arranged it. There is no planetary culling, but they're shipping me out to Bellares on a volunteer pass."

"Which means you volunteered."

"It's what I want, Starry Highness, for now. If I survive—"

"Few do."

"— I'll have a clan-name and a future."

"That could happen sooner than you think, boy; I am a Princeling; I do have lines of communication with the High Inquest; surely they would grant me a small favor...."

"No, Starry Highness. Let me go through the system. Let me achieve on my own merits, even if I die trying."

"Admirable."

The acolytes, priestesses, servocorpses, matrons and the Goddess now rose, and waited for their ruler to speak.

"Now, Goddess," he said. "Is it not true that we've not had religion on this world for centuries, and that all these rituals are just that ... ceremonies performed for the sake of tradition, not out of belief?"

"It could be seen that way," the Goddess said.

"And I am not, as Princeling of the World Entire, and Lord of Nevéqilas, the titular head of all religions, not needing any process of council, senatorial vote, or juristic debate to exercise that power?"

"Yes, Starry Highness. Religion comes under your direct command."

"In that case, I decree that mutilations will no longer be performed in the Temple of Aërat without the consent of the acolyte, who shall receive three counsellings before granting such consent; that such counsellings will com-prise not only religious advisors but members of fields outside religion: mind-healers, cultural anthropol-ogists, rememberers. Smoothening will not be banned per se, but it should be performed only on those who believe. Let it be this moment recorded that the Laws of the World are altered to reflect this."

"The boy shall be sent to Bellares, the childsoldier training world, on my personal transport," he continued. "Mikkálu, you shall kiss Éluma goodbye; it may be that, with time dilation in space travel, you will never see her again."

Mikkálu embraced Éluma, a little awkwardly; she said to him, "I won't forget you."

And he said, "You're the only person in this place who ever smiled at me."

In the Labyrinth of Shadows, one half smile and one defiant conversation were an entire relationship: the meeting, the connection, the crisis, the breakup.

And then I-don't-know was gone. They were all gone. All but she and Princeling. They were alone together. And she ran to his arms. She could not understand what had happened, did not want to understand; she knew only that all she had ever known was broken and that this man might put it back together again.

"Why didn't they tell me?"

Orifec said, "Ah but in the final tests, the clients are always real."

"Clients, indeed ... but you ... you could simply summon anyone you wish. ..."

"I am not my father, nor my grandfather ... though I was born from a doppling kit, I'm not just a copy of a dead ruler," he said. "Maybe the Princeling who succeeds me must also be cloned from my flesh, but why shouldn't I know love, children, the lives of normal people? Oh, but you hardly now me. You don't know that I walk the streets in disguise, night after night, listening to what the people have to say. Éluma, I will establish you in a house of your own in the city; I would like to visit you sometimes; I would not like you to be half a human being, made "smooth" to be a canvas on which to paint my fantasies; perhaps we shall even decide to make a child together.

"Oh, look, Éllekeh, there is something they forgot, in their haste." The tray of prosthetics lay on the floor, but among them was something black, perhaps alive; it was a fabric so sheer that it could not be seen, yet it obscured that which it covered. Orifec pulled it from the tray. "Feel it. It's your cloak of shadow."

He draped the sheet of nothing around Éluma's shoulders. She was well aware of the cloak's symbolism. As a priestess of Aërat, she would have been sworn to remain always in the shadow of the one who paid for her love. She would never have questioned the client, for his desires were inviolable, even, for the right price, to the point of death. But this man, who held the power of life and death over everything in this world, she did dare question. That was a new and disturbing feeling.

"If you had a child who was not you," she said to him, "he would not rule. He would be something quite different. What would you have him be?"

The Starry Highness thought for a moment, then pulled her to him. Kissed her forehead very gently. She saw herself disappear beneath the shifting cloak of shadow. "I've always loved music," he said.

Six
In a Glass Garden

Two boys entered an awakening city, in search of a woman cloaked in shadow.

Two boys entered a city that was still constructing itself, knitting itself into shape like a living thing, sucking in the old capital and absorbing it unto itself, as the people bins continued to disgorge the world's new citizens.

It was night and a very long night, too, for many people bins were still in orbit, shadowing the sunlight. It was cold. The new city was all spindles and cogs and threads of metal flinging themselves across the sky as they wove themselves into walls. Buildings grew from seedlings and storefronts bloomed where there had just been a mass of writhing metal. Streets were haphazard; the city had an air of having been improvised ... like the opening *alap* of an epic song.

They took care not to be seen together; when one ran into the light, the other stood in the shadow of an alley. Presently they found them-selves in a street that spiraled round and round toward a central circular plaza, and there were always doorways to hide in, and so many people bustling about that it was easier not to be noticed.

The people around them wore unfamiliar clothes. Their colors were garish, the fashions outlandish. Most seem to know where they were going. It seemed that the new city had been programmed around the city they had left. Sajit saw a man with several children go up to a door and when he placed his palm against it, it irised open to admit him.

Tijas said, "This city is a sort of doppling of its own, it's their old city, close to it, and the homes open up to them when they read their DNA."

"So we will be homeless."

"Unless we find someone generous."

"Quiet now. I have a plan."

Sajit sent Tijas to sit in the shadow of a fountain. He found a spot a tenth-klomet away, a bit of clearing; he stood in the clearing and he began to sing.

He sang not a song in the highspeech, but one from Attembris, in the dialect of the world that was being cannibalized all around them.

The song was no more than a ditty, really, a simple thing about a village lad who loved a girl who appeared only when the moons sang.

People began to stop and listen.

A gipfer clinked at his feet. A half-gipfer, presently a handful of the coins ... finally an arjent.

He went on singing, his voice shaking.

Until he felt a rough hand on his shoulder. The coins on the flagstones were being scooped up. And a gruff voice. "You need a license for that, brother!"

"Let him sing," a woman said. "It's a pretty song."

The man let go. When Sajit looked up, he did not see much; a beard, flushed cheeks, striated in the intermittent light of the fountain.

"I didn't know I needed a license to sing," Sajit said.

The man laughed now, a hearty laugh. "You don't," he said. "Unless I say you do. And you're taking all our business."

Sajit saw other entertainers in the plaza now. Someone was juggling small rodents. In another corner someone was hammering away at planks to set up a makeshift servocorpse theater.

"Just pick a different corner." The man was whistling now to a troupe of acrobats. "But wait ..." he said. "Do you have an instrument? They move far better to a solid beat."

"I —"

"What about that other boy you are with? The one skulking in the shadows with his face always downcast? Ho, come our of there!"

"He's very shy."

Too late! The woman who had admired his singing had grabbed Tijas by the hand and was pulling him toward them. "You can't look at him!" Sajit whispered harshly. "You can't!"

The man looked at both of them. "Why not?"

"Because he's a doppling!"

"What's that?"

"An abomination — a thing that must be destroyed —" Sajit felt tears spurting.

"So, you've a twin," said the man.

"What's a twin?" Tijas said.

The woman said, "They're from Urna, you idiot!."

"Urna? Where – oh, the world we accidentally displaced. Yes, sorry about that. Supposedly these mistakes never happen, but it's a *very* large galaxy and we are just backworlds."

The woman said, "Daro, twins are *haram* on this world." using a lowspeech term Sajit had never heard.

"I see. A bit of a culture clash." He pulled Tijas and Sajit together and looked from one to the other. Tijas flinched when the woman tried to put her arm around his shoulder. But Sajit saw now these people did not react in the expected way. They seemed to be inured to the sight of abomination.

"Twins all right. A planetary taboo. Poor boys, I imagine you must have been shunned all your lives. No longer! And you probably both play and sing. In some parts of the Dispersal, you'd have been sold to some mighty lord by now. Wouldn't they, Zelma?"

The woman called Zelma, whose eyes were painted with rainbow dust, said, "You must forgive him boys. He's ... a lout. Daro, twins are *haram* on Urna, which is senseless, but on Urna, they don't have slaves. They only use dead people. Which is actually rather advanced of them."

Tijas looked across the square, where the theater was completed now, and a slapstick comedy was in progress, with a fat lady bashing a three-armed man with a toy club while children giggled. His eyes went wide with astonishment.

"You mean those actors are living people?"

Daro said, "It seems that our societies, shoved together by some misplaced decimal point in the calculus of the High Compassion, could never have naturally arisen on the same planet."

"Rubbish. Old Earth had plenty of variant societies."

"And now," said Daro, "Professor Zelma moves from science to mythology. There is no such place."

"Then where did the human race come from?"

Sajit said, "Can we have our money, please? We need food and somewhere to stay."

Daro thought a moment, then flung the tokens back to Sajit. "Let us begin properly," Zelma said. "I am Nar Zelma z'Tarovén, Professor of Pre-Dispersal Research at the University of Kurremkurráh."

"You have a clan-name!" Sajit said in wonder.

"... for what it's worth. I was doing research on Alykh when the people bins came."

"And I," Daro said, "and Daro-without-a-Clan, a juggler and entertainment mogul. I am also the Professor's ... secretary. Bodyguard. Paramour."

"And we are Sajit and Tijas-without-Clans. We are looking for a woman cloaked in shadow."

"A sacred whore of Aërat!" Zelma said. "How I would love to interview her for my research."

"These twins are lucky for us," Daro said.

"How?" Sajit said. "We're — what did you call it — *haram* in this world. And we're homeless and hungry."

"We have nowhere to stay either," Daro said. "Not *officially*. We're not actually *from* ... what is the name of that planet?"

Zelma said, "Alykh."

"Oh yes. The pleasure world."

"Where we thought we could pick up a sack of arjents, on the way home! And look what happened!

Time-frozen, dropped off on a planet even more barbaric than the one we were visiting!"

In a short time, Sajit's world had changed from a village to a city to a great planet and now two planets, with glimpses of yet more worlds....

Tijas said, "These people don't seem to care ... that we are dopplings."

"No," Zelma, "why should we? After all the worlds we have seen? But you should still be careful. It may be that Alykh shares your superstitions. Most of these worlds do ... I mean the *irrational* planets ... the ones with primitive beliefs, with gods and demons ... there's something frightening about twins to many barbarian societies."

Sajit said, "Urna's not barbarian. We stopped believing in the gods centuries ago...."

"Yet you have temples. ..." Zelma said, smiling a little.

"Ruined. Disused."

"Ghosts do not die all at once," said Daro. "Come, we will take you somewhere. One of you ..." He pulled a shawl from Zelma's shoulder a threw it over Tijas's head. "A precaution, Professor. We don't want any witch hunts."

"Where are we going?" Tijas said.

"Food and lodging. For the taking!" Daro laughed and dragged Sajit behind him, and Zelma took Tijas's arm and they set off down a side street.

***

And many years before that day, another boy heard the soft pounding on his coffin-womb and knew that it was time for birth and death.

He did not know how long he had been there, because time in amniosis there is no time as such; he was being fed the memories, the histories of all those who had borne his DNA since the first Orifec ruled on Urna. And he knew what was expected of him when the the time would come for him to emerge.

Urna was an old world, settled, indeed, before the very existence of the Dispersal of Man. When the Inquest came, all planetary norms were kept in place; and Orifec-within-the-Womb saw it all unfold; the founding of Nevéqilas, the War of the Elephantines, the burning of the temples of Gön; the sight of the tachyon bubbles raining from the sky, signalling the acceptance of Urna into the Dispersal; all these things he saw as if with his own eyes.

He saw himself emerge, grow old, from age to age, and knew how one Orifec succeeds another; so when, after a time that was outside time, there came a knock on side of the box, and he heard a priest intone words in a dead language that only he remembered, he knew what he must do.

First there was a light. The amniostuff still clung to his flesh. He stepped forth, and as he knew he would, found himself stand-ing before the Princeling's deathbed.

He already knew where this would be.

In Nevéqilas there was a secret garden called Véra-vur, a garden made of glass. The garden could be reached only through displacement. It had no door and its walls were holo-sculpts of itself, so that the garden went on foreverm without even a horizon; above, a brightly lit night-scape, for the singing moons of Urna shone altogether, imparting a soft glow to the air.

Millions of smooth glass pebbles comprised its floor, and rising from the glittery cold sea were twisted outcroppings, handblown fantastical shapes, many taller than a man.

In the center of the glass garden there grew a single tree, one whose crystal fronds spread out, to form a circle of shade; the glass leaves tinkled in the wind. And under the shade of the tree was the deathbed, a square of pure air that allowed the old princeling to hover in a field of nothing, so no cloth could scrape against raw skin.

The Garden of Glass was where the Starry Highnesses went to die.

On the bed lay he himself, a much older version at any rate; hairless, withered, thin. On either side stood a councillor, a man and a woman, each cloaked in clingfire and the feathers of phoenixes.

Orifec-within-the-Womb stepped forward — he could barely walk yet, but he knew he must do this all by himself.

Orifec-of-the-Past beckoned to him with a weak finger. "Sit beside me. You will find the bed easily enough, or it will find you." His voice was dry and creaky, like an old door in a cold wind.

Sure enough, the bed found him, just when he thought he might collapse. The cushiony air caught him as he was about to fall and oozed around him, and it carried him to sit beside his dying doppling.

"Welcome, Orifec-within-the-Womb," said the old man. He was unclothed. There were two child-servo-corpses kneeling beside him, and they were already anointing his body with the burial-ointment. The smell of it was cloying, ripe. "Are you ready?"

"Can it not wait, Starry Highness?" For he was terribly afraid; he had been in the world of the living for only a few minutes, and he was already being asked to despatch his predecessor to the land of the dead.

"You don't want to kill me." The old princeling laughed. "I understand. I was the same way. But this is the moment. I chose it. It is with complete equanimity and without regret that I close this chapter of our rulership."

Two more aides stepped forward now. They took a

tiny worm from a dish, and placed the worm on the old Princelings forehead. "This creature has been bred to be a conduit of data," explained an aide, "whether from thinkhive to thinkhive, or from brain to brain."

The aide pulled at the worm and it began lengthening. He motioned for Orifec-within-the-Womb to lean over and he dragged the wiry worm until it touched the base of Orifec's skull. He felt a pinprick as it burrowed.

The Elder Princeling said, "I bequeath you all that remains of me; my life story, my hopes, my dreams, my secrets."

Information began to flood his mind. Trysts and whispers. Judgments and desires. In the womb, he had rehearsed for this moment, again and again, and he knew he must dissolve the barrier between himself and the others. The waves of information came. And at the center of all this was the knowledge ... the dark know-ledge ...

I had a brother once....

***

The quarters were not exactly what Sajit was used to. It was a single room, accessible through a mechanical door with hinges — Sajit did not know such doorways still existed. It did not read anyone's palm. It had a doorknob.

He had been frustrated by it a few times until Daro told him that it twisted one way to open, the other way to close.

It wasn't a room for people, but a storeroom for *zul;* thus it was always cool, and the walls and floor were lined with real wood. Vats of various vintages lined the walls. "We might starve," said Daro, "but we shan't want for drink."

There were about a dozen here; some acrobats, a magician, a storyteller.

"More freeloaders!" said one of them, smirking. "Will you pimp them out?"

Daro said, "Alykh will be reestablished within a hundred sleeps. And when Alykh reforms itself …"

"The *dorezdas* will follow. And we'll be squeezing every gipfer we can," Zelma said.

"Dorezdas?" Tijas said.

"They are what pays the bills. The wander from world to world, taking their plea-sure and paying for it well."

"We'll need money if we are to go home."

"Home!" the acrobat scoffed. "Yes! In stasis in the hold of a delphinoid … who knows what century it will be if we ever got there."

"Home is not the place you are from," Sajit said. "It is the place in your heart, the place that calls to you, that you can never reach."

Words from an old *qazel*.

Zelma said, "See? These boys aren't just pretty faces. They could make us all rich. And they're fugitives us all — like us. This is another world with the Twin Taboo — if they're caught, at least one will die."

And Daro said, "Sing for them, Sajit."

Sajit said, "I'll sing the whole song. It's called *The Homeworld of the Heart*. But first I must tune my whisperlyre."

***

It was a tennight before he came to her, and when he came, at first he said nothing. The door dis-solved and he was there, and he strode in and seized her by her slender waist and crushed her lips with his. She could barely breathe. She was almost choking, and then, ab-ruptly, he stopped.

"Éluma," he whispered. "I'm sorry to come to you like this."

He let go. He went to sit on a hoverpillow that rose from the floor to receive him.

"You may come as you wish, Starry Highness," Éluma said. "You are my Lord. My flesh, my soul … take what you wish."

"No," Orifec said. "That is your training, your endless exercises in compliance. But how would your training hold up if you saw who I really am?"

"You're a king."

"I murdered my brother. My father. My uncles. My grand-fathers."

"I don't think so, my Lord. There's been no talk of royal murders, ever. News would reach even the Temple of Aërat, I am sure."

"No, I don't mean I, this human body, physically did it. But I have all their memories, you know. I can't escape the centuries of bloodshed. Every Starry Highness from the beginnings of our world is in me."

"I am also trained to listen," Éluma said. "You'll find that I listen well."

But Orifec was weeping. She put her arms around him and comforted him as she imagined a mother might comfort a child, though the only mothers who ever had ever comforted her were well-programmed servo-corpses. Their programming must have been well thought out indeed, for Orifec grew still at her touch.

And said, "You held me like a child."

And she said, "You could tell."

He answered, "Yes, I could, though no one ever held me that way except a servocorpse."

It was then that Éluma discovered what they had in common, the princeling and the prostitute; they had both been orphaned. Not through death, but through vicious circumstance, through accident of birth; Éluma's mother's need for cash, Orifec's rôle as supreme ruler of a backworld.

And so they made love, each seeing in the other, perhaps, a different person from the one who was there, a fantasy person; yet their need was such that the imagined impinged on the real.

And each time they met, Éluma learned a fresh fragment of Orifec's ancient memories. The fratricide, the sentencing of whole generations of his family to gruesome slaughter, the stabbing of an infant, the hurling of a household into a fiery pit ... and finally ... to the pact that kept the peace: the Starry House would reproduce only by the for-bidden means of doppling, each doppling to emerge and replace his predecessor at the moment of the latter's passing; a planet's peace at the price of a princeling's abomination.

"I remember slitting the baby's throat." Orifec said. "I remember it every day. There's a whistling sound that goes with it."

"That's was centuries ago."

"I know. That's why, with you, I want to be the not-Orifec. I want the borders of Urna to end at the entrance to this room. I want a child."

She gasped. Stifled the gasp immediately; a priestess of Aërat was allowed no private emotions. Never showed surprise at a client's demands.

"You would undo those centuries of stasis?"

"Call it a flaw that happened after they copied the same strand of DNA so many times ... but I don't want to be me. I want a child...."

Éluma said, "But we'd have to rear it in secret...."

***

And the boy who once performed for a princeling sang in the town square, under the singing moons, sang for a song; at first only a few locals came, and the singing was a prelude to some other performance: the troupe specialized in historico-myth dramas, and presented its own version of *The Tale of Mother Vara* with great slickness, though it was a worn old story.

Most often Sajit would per-form, as overture, the folk song called *Woman and Thinkhive,* about a massive machine who loves a human woman.

It is a simple song, simple lyrics, simple-minded; a dialogue between the heart and the head, each wanting to possess the other.

Sometimes Tijas would sing, and Sajit would be hidden backstage, sometimes wearing a mask, ready to come on as an extra. *Mother Vara* is a very basic kind of story; a woman lands on a planet, the planetary thinkhive falls in love with her, together they rule the galaxy; she leaves; the thinkhive burns out, consumed by grief.

Stretching out so plain a story arc to last for several sleeps, like a good street opera should, required inventive incidents, improvised comedy, a dash of juggling, a lot of acrobatics, and long interludes of song while the cast changed their clothes.

At first there were only locals, but soon some who had survived the collapse of Shirénzang came creeping to this vibrant new metropolis. They could be recognized by their monochromatic garb and the way they walked; it was not brazen like the people of Alykh.

In twenty sleeps word came that a starport had built itself a hundred klomets from the city, grown from a seedling, sucking the metals from the earth until it could fashion them into the pillars, parapets and platforms of a city in the sky.

"Any day now," Daro said, "the *dorezdas.*"

But the drama continued, day after day. Professor Zelma herself took the role of Mother Vara, who according to legend was the first ... and will be the last ... Inquestor. Tijas and Sajit, alternating on and offstage, sometimes had lines in the play, composed in a curious singsongy style, in a very basic pidgin that made it presumably easy to understand no matter what world the drama was performed on:

> Dara muzherwo
> Patia Kuerwo
> Ma Pannusi kwe
> De Patiwe khnerwo...

"Star woman pain in heart; but thinkhive not pain...."

An evening came when Sajit was singing this very song. The crowd was thin. His whisperlyre jangled, the sympathetic strings being out of alignment, but knowing this Sajit exploited the tonal dissociation to distinguish finer and finer *shrutas,* allowing his voice to play with microtonal inflections too subtle, perhaps for such a folk melody.

The audience was by no means under his spell — perhaps the day would come when he could pluck one string and hypnotize a planet, but this was not that day. And yet, and yet ... there *was* someone watching him intently.

A performer knows when he is being watched.

Instinctively, as his lips and vocal chords form the notes, as he fingers seek out the strings, his eye follows the path of observation and he knows where the interest is coming from.

All he could see were eyes, because the man was enveloped in the skin of a gray marsupial. A look of recognition passed between them.

Sajit returned to his song, and when he looked again, the man was gone.

***

"Tijas —"

It was night in the very crowded storeroom. Stale sweat and rancid *zul* in the air. And snoring. But Sajit and Tijas almost always could find somewhere a little apart: a sack, a barrel, a metal chest. It was not like the amnio-hammock back home but it was a kind of privacy. It helped that they were still small, small for their age, even.

The costume department of Daro's troupe doubled as their bedding. Tonight they had managed to cadge the imperial fur of Lord Kárdovany, because the actor who played that role had fallen into a *zul*-induced stupor. It was not real, but it was still soft.

Tijas would always fall asleep more quickly. *I'm the worrying one,* Sajit thought, *because I've lived the full years of my age, and I've known the comfort of my village, before it was all ripped away.* Sajit had slept badly since their world had collapsed. For Tijas, the new world was no newer than the old. It was an adventure.

Tijas wanted to sleep but he could sense Sajit's urgency ... that empathy, the ability to read each other's thoughts, if anything was strengthening now. "What is it?" Tijas said.

"I've seen Arbát," Sajit said. "He must have survived."

"Did you speak to him?"

"No. He didn't want to be seen."

"Maybe we should let him be."

"No, Tijas. I can't. I've known him as long as I can remember ... strange as he is."

"Sajit ... we have shelter now. We have a place to sleep and they're nice to us. When they save up enough to get off the planet —"

"We have to find Arbát. We have to find ... the woman. Maybe he knows her. All the time I was growing up, things were going on that people hid from me. I need to know these things."

"Why, Sajit?"

"Because they're part of who I am. Don't you understand it, Tijas? I — we — are going to be a writer of songs. To know the art, first know thyself."

"The *Aphorisms of Arbát,* disk one, number one."

"Let's go exploring tomorrow, after the play. We won't be missed."

"Tomorrow. But now, we'll sleep."

But Sajit could not, and presently he retrieved the ring from the pouch where he always kept it, and sat there, turning it this way and that, catching the cold room's pallid light. Eventually se saw that Tijas was shivering in his sleep, so he put his arms around his doppling to warm him, and lay there with his eyes open until dawn.

Seven
An Unexpected Ally

He held the child in his arms for only a few minutes, before he started to be afraid. In fact he was shaking.

"Don't be nervous," she said to him, "you're not going to break him."

"*Break* him?"

He seemed even more troubled, so she took the baby. He started to cry but she rocked him, singing a half-remembered lullaby ...

Sleep, child, sleep;
The Inquestors are watching you
from their far heaven.

The wings of pteratygers are fanning you;
The war is done.
Your mother's arms are warm.

Sleep, child, sleep.

And she thought: *How do I know this song? What mother held me in her arms? Whose voice was it? Was it just some singing holosculpt?*

But the boy grew still. "He's quiet now. I'm glad

you came today; you haven't named him yet."

"I —"

"You're afraid to name him, even afraid to touch him."

Orifec said, "It's the memory. I held a child like this once. I slit its throat. I can feel the sticky blood. I can smell it. My own brother." His eyes gazed at ghosts.

Éluma knew the story from ancient history, knew how long ago it happened; but to the Princeling it was the immediate past; she could see that. "It was stupid of me to think I would be the one to change everything...."

"But you have changed. You wanted a relationship with a woman, a *real* woman. You wanted a child."

"Is this a relationship? Or is it an artifice created by your perfect training?" And Éluma could not answer him, did not know what separated her truth from her art.

Instead, she said, "You wanted this child so much, you wanted so much to challenge your ancestry —"

"I had a dream that everything could be different his time."

His dream is fracturing, she thought.

The next thing to go, perhaps, would be his love. If indeed it *was* love.

She subvocalized a brief command, intensifying the pheromonal generators in the chamber. She dimmed the lighting, made it more warm. She called up a soft zephyr. The love nest was fully equipped. These subtle shadings of the ambience were designed to calm an overanxious lover, but Orifec became more aggravated.

"It's true," he said. "I'm afraid of ... breaking him."

"What do you want to do?"

"I want to ... I want him to be safe. I want to care for him, but ..."

"Starry Highness, he has a destiny."

"Yes. But not a royal one."

"He must be protected. As you ... protect me."

But Éluma wondered how much longer that protection would last.

Orifec said, "If you only knew — what goes through my mind — when I hold him."

"Perhaps if you named him, you wouldn't be so afraid."

"When he looks at me, his eyes seem to stab my heart."

She smiled. "Hyperbole."

"No, no. I feel real pain. Because there's something else I see...."

And he told her. *Childsoldiers.* One day the Inquest would come, and they would take all the best, the cleverest, the ones with the best reflexes. And their eyes would be fitted with laser-irises, so that their very glance would be death. "We can't let them take him."

"I thought you wanted him to be a musician," she said. And wiped a tear from his eye with a gentle finger.

"And so he shall be. And the powers of powers will witness: I'll protect him even if I have to break every law in the world. His name shall be Sajit — in the high-speech, 'the arrow that flies true,'" said Orifec.

"Because he wounds you when he looks at you."

"Yes, yes."

Éluma kissed him, and his lips grew cold, and she was afraid. But he was the Princeling. There were things she could never say to him. Not ever.

***

... and Arbát was there again.

Evening ... moons dancing over the square ... a whispering fountain ... the start of a magical night. A few *dorezdas* already: their off-world garb, their undulating wigs, their jagged jewelry, gawking at everything and everyone.

Sajit was onstage, masked, in a crowd scene. It was Tijas who was strutting on the flagstones, his high voice modulating and setting the sympathetic strings of his whisperlyre to a shimmery vibration.

Tijas was in fact being a little naughty. The simple folk melodies they had to sing was a bit too straight-forward and he had launched into an endless cadenza, mixing his shrutas from different scales and shamelessly improvising in a style that probably have made Arbát pull out the strap, *for the singer must ever be subordinate to the song....*

Except that Arbát was there. Tijas had not noticed him. But Sajit, stuck in a frozen tableau in front of which Mother Vara was wildly emoting, could see Arbát clearly; could see that he was resisting the impulse to reveal himself and teach the boy a lesson right then and there.

When Tijas had come to a caesura in the music, Sajit tried to send him a mental message — sometimes this worked like magic, sometimes it didn't at all — and this time he definitely felt Tijas physically shudder, felt the shud-der in his own body, almost tripped from his precarious position in the tableau. Both of them saw Arbát try to slip away unnoticed.

The play had a long duologue between Vara and the thinkhive which had been known to gone for several hours; it was about to begin, so Sajit slipped away and met Tijas behind the stage. The two boys hooded themselves and pulled polarizing veils down over their faces.

"He went north," Tijas said. "That's the direction of the Old City."

"There are new displacement plates," Sajit said. "They go in a straight line."

They wrapped their hoods and cloaks about them tighter, loosened their polarizing veils so that they no longer hugged their faces; they became like moving shadows, unrecognizable. The shadows grew longer. They left the square, taking the northern path.

In only a few steps they had passed a forest, a transport hub, an empty field, an auto-latifundium, and a long tall wall that was still under construction, with metal spiders crawling up and down and disgorging liquid amalgam that wove itself into great glistening skeins of gold and iridium, translucent to the moonlight. There were few people.

... and then they saw him.

He was standing at a low stone entrance. The walls were holosculpt to blend with a surrounding orchard, so it seemed that the entrance was an arch-way in the midst of a landscape. Only the fact that people were going in and out, and vanishing when they entered, betrayed the artifice.

"Stay concealed," Sajit said to Tijas. They crept closer. There was a *gruyesh* tree whose branches provided shadow and they could see Arbát clearly.

Arbát stood patiently as others went in an out. Presently there came a servocorpse ... in the brown skinrobe of a pleasurer. It spoke in a voice neither male nor female, and its body had elements of both.

The corpse said, "Welcome. We offer pleasure with the dead and the living. What offering do you have for Aërat?"

"I want an hour with the living."

"Do you bring an appropriate offering?"

"I have only twelve gipfers."

The servocorpse ... almost appeared to be snickering. "You may not buy even the cheapest living acolyte of Aërat ... not even an apprentice ... and not even for a minute. You may forget about the ones who are Cloaked in Shadow!"

"Please ..."

"But the dead are available if you want something quick ... and dirty." The servocorpse seemed to leer. "Twelve gipfers might stretch until dawn; the night is already half gone."

"Take it all."

"Give me the visual and behavioural parameters so that a corpse may be prepared for you."

Arbát fished a holosculpt from his robe and showed it to the procurer-corpse. The corpse nodded and disappeared, presently emerging with a figure shrouded in black crisscrossed with swaths of darkfabric.

"Dressed just like us," Tijas whispered. "Invisible. Not-persons."

The procurer said, "Damage will be paid for."

"I understand."

Arbát began to walk away from the doorway, leading the draped pleasure corpse by the hand. Tijas and Sajit were so close they could almost touch them, but Arbát was too engrossed in private thoughts to see the world.

Presently Arbát stopped. "I have to look at you," he said. He was weeping, uncontrollably weeping. And he pulled down the corpse's face-covering.

Sajit gasped.

"It's *us,*" he thought, and he knew Tijas heard his thought clearly. The boys each clenched the other's hand, feeling a kind of dread ... and a kind of familiarity.

Arbát pulled down the veil but not before the dopplings saw the eyes, grotesquely sculpted to resemble their own ... and the come-hither eyelashes grafted onto the dead flesh. Sajit could feel Tijas grip his hand, so tightly that it hurt.

Then Arbát and the pleasure corpse moved away, towards the first displacement plate.

"Sajit," Tijas said, "he has answers. You weren't there that day ... when I found him ... *bursting the milkpod.*" But Sajit could see that his doppling was terrified and that theirs was not a shared memory. It was a primal trauma that Sajit could not touch, for their were parts of each other's minds that remained locked, however much they wanted to be one person.

***

The entrance to an unpretentious home, the last house in the village, in the shadow of a forest ... many years before ... a Woman Cloaked in Shadow, a child sharing basket with a whisper-lyre....

A childless woman standing in a doorway, a child beginning to cry ...

A woman cloaked in shadow disappearing into the forest.

Moons, dancing in the bright clear night.

***

"I'll go. I saw it before. I know what to expect."

"No, Tijas. *I'll* go. What you saw has hurt you. And if you were hurt, I too want to be hurt. Your world, my world, they *have* to be the same."

The two boys huddled together in the middle of the night, in the storeroom that had become their dwelling, whispering over a cushion of snores.

"No, Sajitteh. We are bound to grow apart, though we sprang from the same helix. Let's keep our private traumas."

"I'll go, Tijasseh, because I'm older. And that's that."

"You take such good care of me, brother." And kissed his doppling on the cheek.

Sajit said, "You're here because someone wanted you to die in my place. That's nor fair."

"I'm your dop-pling. You came before me. I owe you who I am."

"Who taught you to say that?"

"I don't know. When I lay in amniosis, unborn, I think the doppling kit imprinted me."

"Then you'll do as I say."

"Of course."

"And it's my turn to wear the ring."

Tijas fished it from his tunic and hung it around his doppling's neck.

The ring! Sajit touched it now. The intaglio was warm, not icy-cold like the day the Starry Highness had closed Sajit's fingers around it.

"Do you think it's alive?" Sajit said, thinking of the double-serpent columns in the royal chamber, in the old time.

But Tijas was already asleep.

***

And so Sajit stepped out of the copse, a few sleeps later, having tracked Arbát once more to the gateway of the Temple of Aërat. Arbát was striding toward the entrance. He did not have a chance to enter; Sajit intercepted him.

"No need to enter," he said. "I am already here."

"But I wish to —"

"No payment. The —" Sajit began to improvise a little "— thinkhive of the temple has stored your desires in its memory wells. I have been sent."

"But I haven't paid," Arbát said. He was suspicious. So Sajit took him by the hand and with his other hand he lowered his polariser. Arbát gasped.

"What have they done? You look almost like ..."

"I am a more expensive model." Sajit said. "Come."

Arbát was bewildered but Sajit felt a rush of power; the man was entirely his to control. It made him queasy amd strangely excited. *How easily lying comes to me,* he thought. And followed his tutor, step for step, carefully remaining three steps behind, like an obedient corpse.

Presently they came to a dingy room. It was accessible only by displacement plate, so Sajit could not even tell if he were underground or above it, for there were no windows. The walls did not even have any scenery projected. Unless ... these cracks, that caked-on grime, those creeping insects, were in fact —

They were.

Arbát clapped his hands and the holoscene dissolved. The real walls were white, antiseptic ... and smelled faintly of a chemical used to eliminate pests.

"Forgive me for the unseemly décor," Arbát said. "But I need to be reminded of how I've failed you. Not you, not you of course, you are just animated dead flesh, and yet...."

"Shall I disrobe, sir?" It was a line Sajit remembered from one of Daro's plays.

"You never asked me that before. Before, you knew what I wanted. You would go straight for the laser-quirt and throw me against the wall."

"I'm a different model," Sajit reminded him.

"I suppose I'll ... follow my programming."

There was a bed against the wall. Oddly, it was solid, constructed from biological materials, wood and fabric. It did not rise to contour around the body as he knelt, but stayed quite rigid. Sajit slipped out of his clothes, one piece at a time. He did not know what he should do with the ring around his neck — but, just in time —

"Turn away," Arbát said. "Turn your back. I don't want you to see my face."

Sajit waited, imagining what the old man's hands would feel like on his skin. They had looked dry, flaky even. Obediently he looked at the wall and waited for whatever it was that Tijas had witnessed.

Instead, he heard the twang of a whisperlyre.

"If you won't punish me," he said, "let me punish myself."

And Arbát began to sing.

***

There was a village, Arbát sang. *There was a clearing in the village where a young boy heard the song the moons sang ... and long to sing of the stars and the worlds beyond the world he lived in....*

And one day there came to the forest clearing a woman cloaked in shadow. So close did she wear the shadow that Arbát saw nothing of her face. He saw only a movement, a rustle of the dark.

The woman said to him, A boy is growing up in your village. You will teach him everything you know, and he will become Shen.

Arbát himself had never been named to the Clan of Shen, the masters of song.

The woman said, You will know the boy when he comes to you. He will have an air about him, as of a ruler over worlds, though he be but a humble village child.

And Arbát sang of the boy's halting first notes, of coaxing them into tune, of shading them, of filling them out with words that could touch men's souls....

And Arbát sang of love, love for the thing he dreamed of but could never be, of the self that was not himself, of the longing for a music deeper than music....

***

Orifec had told her, "You'll find the musician in the forest clearing just outside the village. He thinks it is his private secret place ... but actually it's a place our family has always watched. And fine musicians have been born in that clearing before.

"They go there to be alone, because it is a place where the confluence of light and shadow, of wind and moisture, are so well mixed that it seems like the birthplace of a elemental power ... a God, if you like."

She was no musician, but even she could feel the music of the place. The celestial harmony of moons and clouds. The sighing of the wind. The clarity of the air, the scent of the *vangérides* as the night-blooms swayed.

The musician seemed old, but his face might have shown the wear and tear of a tortured life; she had imagined him a more vigorous man when Orifec played her a song cube of an old recital of his.

"Did I startle you?" Éluma said. "I was told I could find a man named Arbát here."

"I am Arbát." A serious face. Perhaps she had disturbed his rêverie.

"I have a message for you from someone ... in a high place. I don't dare say his name, but this sachet may give you a clue." And what she handed him was a small purse sealed with the double-serpent knot. "I can tell you that it contains a single ozmion. I should not have been able to carry a thousand arjents by myself. No, no, don't unseal it. Trust me."

"I have a rich admirer?" Arbát said. Had some prince picked up a song cube from the souk?

"In a manner of speaking," she said. "This money is a teaching fee. You are to take a special interest in someone. A boy. A boy who is growing up in your village, a boy with a strange destiny. A destiny beyond your own, Arbát-without-a-Clan, for he will become Shen one day."

"How will I know him? I teach many boys in the village. Some, I am sure, are special. Though they're mostly lazy and reluctant; music lessons aren't a high priority in Attembris."

Éluma said, "You will know, Arbát. He'll have an air about him."

Arbát said, "There isn't a treasure-house in this village that would let me exchange an ozmion without asking questions."

She laughed. "Then you'll just have to hang on to it," she said, "in the hope that my master will let you trade it in for a sack of arjents."

***

Sajit remembered his first meeting with Arbát ... it had not gone well.

As Arbát sang in the shabby little room, as he knelt on the bed, naked, facing the wall, as Arbát expounded his life's small indignities in tremulous tones, Sajit remembered —

The room with dozens of students, all cross-legged on a rigid floor, their keening voices tracing the outlines of a raga free of ornament or pitch-bending *shrut,* and he a tiny boy already knowing there was a wrongness in the music. And he was standing in the back of the schoolroom and suddenly he found his own voice swelling, blending yet arcing high above the others in an improvised descant, the melismas colorizing the plain raga so suddenly it was no barren up and down but a rich orchard, a garden, a flowering field —

And then he found himself singing alone, for

the master had cut them all off. His voice sounded thin to him, raspy even. He was ashamed but he went on singing because in his head there was a perfect arc of sound and he needed to complete it.
...
When he finished, the young singers did not applaud, but muttered over and over the sound *mut-mut, shrut-shrut*, which is the highest compliment a singer can receive. Sajit's cheeks flushed.

"I'm sorry, sir," he whispered.

"All of you, be quiet. Our friend has done well. He makes music not out of thin air, but out of an eternal music that he hears, a music that plays deep within, a music you must reach out to catch before it is already gone. Come forward, boy."

Sajit stepped forward, expecting some reward. But as he approached Arbát, the master struck him across the back with a edged ferrule. Sajit screamed.

Arbát said, "This is your first lesson. It's about the song, not the singer. Ne-ver come before me like this, puffed up with pride, thinking you already know the secrets of the cosmos!"

Sajit began to weep. His parents had never hit him. He sobbed, passionately, thinking that it was all over now. But as he wiped his tears with a sleeve, he saw what the whole class had seen the entire time he had been absorbed in his singing and not noticing the world ... he saw that Arbát, too, wept.

***

Sajitteh, Arbát sang, *I taught you with blows, I taught you with harshness and tears ... and where are you now? From*

the moment you first sang, you wounded me and the wound has never healed.
I shall never be what you will become. I knew it in that moment.
I shall never touch the silences between the stars.
When I am old I will sing by the side of the road and the dorezdas will throw me a gipfer or two, and I will waste away....

But Sajit could not contain himself anymore.

"It's not true, Master Arbát!" he cried.

And he could not help himself, he turned away from the wall to face his old teacher, knowing that Arbát would see the ring. Knowing that the pretense must end.

"You're not a corpse —"

"No! What dead thing would know your name? What servo-corpse would weep so much to see his master's weeping?"

"I am sorry. I am so ashamed. I did not want you to know ... how deeply ... I have loved you. When I beat you, when I scolded you ... I loved you."

"There is nothing to be ashamed of, Arbát."

"You knew, didn't you? You spied on me that day."

That was Tijas, Sajit thought. But he said nothing.

"I thought you were dead," Arbát said. "I thought of all the unsung songs, the unwritten poems. Every night I dreamed about you crushed by a crashed cathedral, sliced into cauterized wafers by a child-soldier's eyes."

"Truly, master, there is nothing to be ashamed of."

And Sajit flung himself at his teacher, hugging him hard. They wept until there were no tears left, and only when morning came did Sajit remember his doppling, waiting in the crowded storeroom, waiting to fall asleep in his brother's arms.

***

And there was the ring.

"We have to find her," Sajit said. "She knows things. She knows who I am really am."

"We will have to search," Arbát said, "in the Labyrinth of Love."

***

The ring....

The clasp of a banker's sachet ...

Fifty tennights had gone by and the woman cloaked in shadow stood with another payment in the clearing.

"Who are you?" Arbát said. "Who has sent you? Who is the boy?"

As she had been told to do, Éluma only smiled, and girded up the cloak of darkness, and returned to her waiting auto-kiniton, a wave of darkness undulating in the patchwork of moonlight and trees' shadow.

But the next time they met, Éluma said, "I wish I could see him. From a distance. Just once."

***

The ring....

Tijas felt the ring grow warm against his chest as he lay in the dark room. And yet it was Sajit who was wearing it.

Tijas felt the hot tears spurting down his cheeks, though he was not weeping.

He felt the gnarled hands of an old man against the skin of his back, though he was clothed, though the man was far away.

And he felt empty.

That was the dark side of being so close to his doppling, sometimes feeling his very thoughts, certainly his moods, often his pain.

When he felt these things, and he knew something was happening to Sajit, and he could not be there....

It's a level of aloneness no one can feel, not unless they too have a doppling.

He could not sleep. Until it was dawn, and Sajit was kneeling beside him, telling him of all he'd heard.

"Tijas, Tijas ... we have answers. Well, sort of answers." He started to tell his doppling all he had experienced that evening, but it came out in a jumble: Arbát had known the woman cloaked in shadow from the beginning ... there was a sachet with money, sealed with the same sigil as was depicted on the ring ... and on the whisperlyre.

"I think he knows how to find her," Sajit said. "He mentioned ... the *Labyrinth of Love*."

"A brothel!" said Tajis, gleaning the word from the store of information that had been pumped into him during his long gestation inside the doppling kit.

"She's a whore. Or a priestess. Or a goddess. I am sure she is our mother," Sajit said.

"*Yours*, you mean," Tijas said bitterly.

Eight
To Find the Voice

Our mother....

This was really the first big gulf between them. Sajit had had a family ... and a dark secret this family had not even known in detail ... another mother, the mother who bore him.

Tijas's womb was a wooden box.

Tijas had memories, of course; but his thinkhive-designed mind could not know the things that happened in the outside world, after his seed had been implanted in the box. He and his doppling had shared so much since he had been awakened, could know each other's pain and to some extent each other's thoughts. But sharing was in part an act of will. Each soul contained a well too deep for the other to drink from ...

... and so it was that Tijas did not feel the loss of his parents and sisters as Sajit did. He hadn't teased the girls when they were tiny, or protected them from bullies in school.

He did not remember the nights in the clearing, listening to the moons and wondering about the hugeness of the cosmos.

The doppling process was not really designed to create a random twin; rather it was to keep alive a single consciousness through ages of rule. There were reasons why this technology was taboo for all except the Princeling of Urna; otherwise people would created copies of themselves for companionship or pleasure, and since such dopplings had no legal status, they would always be seen as less than human, able to be abused or exploited.

Urna was now transmuting itself into Alykh, but dopplings were abomination in this world as well; it had been strange to imagine a world where they were not, a world where "twins", as Daro called them without any prejudice or disgust, were accepted as coequal.

Finding the woman cloaked in shadow was Sajit's obsession; it was not Tijas's.

But Sajit rarely asked what Tijas wanted.

"I think the Labyrinth of Love must be the Temple of Aërat," Sajit was saying as they were setting up for the evening's play.

Today's episode was called *The Heartbreak*. It is when Mother Vara learns that the artificial being, the perfect lover that the think-hive has created to be with her, is not human. The role of Mother Vara was played by Zelma and Daro played the handsome simulacrum.

To portray a machine-made humanoid, Daro was daubing himself with a silvery paint. Then, a second layer of iridescent spray so he could glisten in the synth-light of the makeshift the-ater.

Sajit said, "We'll sneak away during Vara's big dance number. We can easily get to the Temple of Aërat and be back before the play ends in time for our solo."

"*You'll* sneak away," Tijas said. "I'm going to stay here and learn some more lyrics from Daro."

"What for? We'll never need them."

"*You'll* never."

"We're going to find our mother. We're going to find out who we really are."

"Who *you* are. Oh, Sajit, you never listen."

"I always listen. I can't not listen. You're always in my head."

"The part of me that you will listen to."

And so they parted for the evening, unhappy with each other.

***

In a break in the show, Arbát found Tijas by the fountain. Tijas knew him before he even looked up; it was the smell of dream-stuff, faintly overlaid with chocolate.

"There's no need to be so stand-offish," Arbát said. "Not after last night, anyway."

But what happened last night? What had transpired between them, that Arbát seemed to have become so much more intimate?

Arbát said, "You must have thought I was going to violate your delicate little body in some way. But I don't do that ... not even to corpses, who do not possess shame or dishonor. Yes, I thought you were a corpse at first — I did not dare to dream that —" He was weeping again.

Tijas wished he would go away. He was afraid he'd blurt out something and Arbát would guess that he was not Sajit. "I swore to the woman," Arbát said, "that I'd always protect you."

Tijas was about to ask, *What woman?* before realizing. He bit his tongue. They had to change to subject. So Tijas said, "Chocolate."

Arbát put his arm round the boy's shoulders, drew up him from the edge of the fountain. The waters danced, twisted by varigravs into streams that bent and interwove and tied themselves into knots. Two emerald sharklets swam, chasing each other in some mating ritual.

"Chocolate," he said. "In this new place, chocolate is not valued as much as in our old world. They don't say as we do, *na shĕtreín shiklátas* — after the songs comes the chocolate. But I have managed to find a place."

"What happened to the Dro-mek Shiklati?"

"It's a ruin. They're ploughing it over and converting it to a slaughterhouse for hydrobovids. That's something like our river-horses, but juicier. The Alykhi are very much into meat, but they do not understand *shikás*. I will take you...."

Tijas found himself over-coming his resistance, and meekly following Arbát through alleyways that were even now assembling them-selves according to some kind of inanimate DNA. Columns corkscrewing out of pavements, bas reliefs chiselling themselves onto walls. Inscriptions popping up on lintels in a hundred languages, from *bhasháhokh* to bar-barous argots.

The place was little more than a stall hemmed

in by a jeweller and a thinkhive vendor; three or four seat cushions hovered around a central brewing station that was, to Tijas's surprise, not operated by a corpse.

"The human touch," Arbát said. He ordered two beakers of foaming pulped peftifesht topped with a sauce of zul-laced chocolate. Tijas gulped it down, missing the old world, the old life. When Arbát climbed onto the floating cushion and sat beside him, Tijas did not really mind, no longer felt threatened. Whatever had happened between the old man and Sajit had somehow defanged him. "Sajitteh," Arbát said, "we must talk about the Voice."

"What do you mean, Master Arbát?"

"Sing to me. The song you've been singing. In that platitude-filled play that those second-rate actors have been putting on in the quadrangle."

Star woman pain in heart —

"As I thought," Arbát said, just like on stage. "There's nothing there."

Nonsense! Tijas thought. *What a jealous old fart.*

For at the very first whimpering *krachak* of the simple melody, everyone in the chocolate shop had turned to watch him. "I'm good," Tijas said. "I don't know what you mean."

"To be good, and to *know* that you're good — that is indeed greatness," Arbát said, "but to be good — and not to know it — that is genius."

"Master, you're just manipulating words."

"No, no." Arbát gripped the boy by the shoulders. His fingernails dug in. "Star woman pain in heart," he said. "What triteness, what tawdry manipulation of the audience. What pain is in *your* heart? What star gives you the most pain?"

"It's just a simple folk song."

"There are no simple songs."

Arbát held the boy's

face, forced him to look into his eyes. "Tell me if you see pain," he said.

Tijas looked.

He remembered the primal moment when he stumbled on Arbát doing secret, shameful things ... things he should not have seen.

"You see," Arbát said, "I still have things to teach you."

***

Éluma doffed her cloak of shadow and gazed at herself in the still reflecting stream that bisected an inner court-yard of her apartment, miraculously left untouched by the collision of cities.

I am still beautiful, she told herself, *I am still a manifestation of Aërat.*

The central thinkhive of the Temple was attuned to her every subvocalization and it whispered to her in ritual response: *Yes, Goddess, you are beautiful, the most beautiful.*

Since the collision she had not seen Orifec. She wondered if he was safe, if he still retained any of the benefits of being a Princeling, now that his world did not officially exist.

She had seen him just the once, as the cities were colliding. The child, she thought, might be with him.

The child ....

The Temple of Aërat still functioned. Clients came and went, low level clients who could only afford to the lovemaking of the dead; the specialist services of the priests and priestesses, trained to be sensitive to every unspoken desire, every nuance of the client's words and movements ... there was little demand for this.

And none at all for one who had once belonged to a Princeling.

She had attained the summit, only to find she had made herself out of reach.

And though it was completely *haram* to even think it, for a priestess of Aërat was an empty vessel into which others poured their passion, she *missed* Orifec.

She missed the child, too, though motherhood was not strictly permissible. She had seen him only a few times.

As she mused on her reflection and thought about her master and her son, there came a crude knock on the wall. A servocorpse was trying to prevent a man from entering, but as they are not really programmed to disobey, and the man was ill-mannered, it wasn't working.

"Who are you? Don't you know this is the inner sanctum of Aërat?"

"Yeah, and you're the living goddess."

"That I am. One of several." She reached for her cloak of shadow.

"All right," said the man. He wore a beard dyed blue and elaborately woven, and iridescent earrings, and a tunic whose clingfire was fringed with feathers. He was pudgy and he smelled of a spice not known on Urna.

"You're not from this world," she said.

"That depends on your view-point," he said. "I could say the same of you. I am an official of the Tourist Department of the Aïrang City Governance Council. My name is Lang viHurak, I am the administrator for *dorezda* attractions."

"This is a temple, not a theme park," Éluma said.

"Ah yes. We're aware that the former Urna was, in some ways, a more superstitious planet than it will now become. But this world is no longer Urna. It's an unfortunate accident that the world was not properly cleared for repopulation, but these mistakes do happen."

"Do you know where Orifec is?"

"The former government is being debriefed," said Lang vi-Hurak. "As I understand it, a compromise is being negotiated. We'll allow, for the length of one standard human lifetime, renewable by mutual agreement, certain areas of the planet to be isolated as reservations for the survivors of Urna. On condition, of course, that *dorezda* visits are allowed."

"So we're to become a sort of zoo...."

"Please don't put it this way," viHurak said. "Of course, we'll process any would-be immigrants once a system is established. But Alykh is a pleasure planet. Its entire economy is *dorezda*-driven. If you'll forgive me — what shall I call you? Goddess? Madame Priestess? Brothel madam?"

"I am called Éluma-without-a-Clan. Éluma will do."

"Then you will do me the honour of calling me Lang," viHurek said. "On Alykh, most people have just one name; as a member of the governing class, I am blessed with the right to use a patronymic. I'm sure we'll work well together. We're allowing the first trial run in two sleeps ... just a dozen *dorezdas*. They are paying well for the privilege, so your 'Temple' will start receiving some income. Now ... I need a tour. Some background. Quaint rituals? What are your requirements for priesthood? How many humans, how many servocorpses? And most importantly ... is there a menu of services? Prices for penetration, fellatio, fantasy fulfillment?"

She laughed then. Heartily. It was true that her life's work was being reconfigured as a tawdry act for the entertainment of off-worlders, yet there was humor in this. "It seems," she said, "we're going into business."

"May I take the tour now?" said Lang viHurek.

***

Sajit stood at the entrance to the Temple, where he had seen Arbát standing, waiting to be admitted. At length, a servocorpse came to the door.

"I'm looking for a woman," he said, "a woman cloaked in shadow."

"Such women do not exist," the corpse said with a kind of programmed haughtiness, "not for the likes of you.'

"Do I have to pay?"

"It isn't payment, but an offering to Aërat. You can half a beautiful corpse for two gipfers. For one, you can get one with a faint whiff of decay."

"I'm looking for a woman cloaked in shadow. One in particular."

"One in particular! A moppet like you, and already the refined tastes of a Princeling!"

Sajit said, "I do have something to pay." He yanked open his garment to reveal the ring that hung around his neck.

"Why didn't you say so earlier?" said the corpse. "But I may not deal with some of your refulgent splendor. I shall have to fetch someone more senior."

If a servocorpse could reveal alarm, this one appeared to. The next figure to appear at the door was not even dead; apparently the double serpent was worth a human response. He was a bearded man of dark blue hue, so dark it was almost black.

"Master," he said, "we have been expecting you."

"How can that be?" Sajit said.

"Well, we have been expecting the Ring," said the doorman, "and naturally the one who bears it must be of considerable importance."

"Then you'll accept it as payment."

"Oh! No no no no no! That Ring is your key. The pleasures of this place are yours."

"Have you seen Orifec?"

'My Lord! Who would dare gaze upon such a personage? By no means. No one here has laid eyes on the Son of the Starlight, the High Princeling Orifec z'Ur-nasi Tath, hereditary Lord of Nevéqilas, Commander of the World Entire, He Who Answers Only to the High Inquest. Not since, oh, oh, not since ... not since it happened."

"And the woman cloaked in shadow?"

"Ah, you may have your choice of those. Though you do seem a little young for physical congress."

"I won't be needing any congress," Sajit laughed. "But I *do* want to see my mother."

"You will not find her here," said the doorman. "No woman cloaked in shadow may bear a child."

"Yet here I am," Sajit said.

"I have no answer for this conundrum," the doorman said. "But ... come inside for a span. Enjoy a snow-cooled sherbet laced with virgin *zul*. You may not yet be capable of ... any milkpod activities ... but there are plenty of other divertissements. Any there is no need to pay. You carry the insignium of the Princeling, and though there's no princeling in the land any-more, no princeling, no princeling ... yet here in this Temple we do not acknowledge any change...."

The doorman reached out put pulled Sajit through the displacement field.

He sound himself in a vast anteroom. Holosculpts of the goddess stood in niches here and there, many with forever lights burning in front of them, or shrouded in the fumes from joss-sticks. The promised *zul* snowcone arrived on a floating tray. People walked past, but no one spoke. The room echoed with whispers, whispers that spoke of longing, of desire.

"Who should I talk to?" Sajit said.

But the doorman had already vanished.

***

She took through the official through the Labyrinth of Love. The corridors wound and spiralled and seemed to shift location; for the Labyrinth of Love was not a linear design, but grew from nested displacement fields, so that a room was often never in the same place twice.

A link-corpse held aloft a laser-candelabrum. It had preprogrammed with all possible permutations of the labyrinth, and was webbed to the central thinkhive of the Temple; without its gui-dance, Lang viHurek would undoubtedly be lost forever.

"This is a spooky experience, very disorienting," viHurek said. "We of Alykh aren't as used to corpses; we don't use them as servants. A trip through this Labyrinth could be quite a thrill. Perhaps a few tableaux of some of your more unusual ... manifestations of the human mating urge."

"I'm sure we can program some of our spare dead to have pretimed congress on a cycle," Éluma said.

"And congress with the goddess herself, for the sufficiently well-heeled? I mean, my own bureaucratic salary could doubtless not suffice, and yet ... perhaps being allowed to taste the highest delights might make this go a lot more smoothly...."

Éluma couldn't abide this man anymore. "Get out!" she screamed. "You're raping our culture, turning our most cherished beliefs into a sideshow about barbarous superstitions —"

"Just doing my job, Your Divinitude or whatever I'm supposed to call you. You don't want to make my job a little more pleasant, I won't make yours pleasant either."

"It's you who are the savages!" Éluma screamed, and slapped his face.

She was appalled. Aërat does not show personal emotions. Aërat is there only for the devotee. *How could I have slipped?*

Meanwhile, viHurek wasn't letting up. He seized her by the shoulders, yanking away the cloak of shadow.

"No one refuses an official of the Tourist Department," he whispered harshly.

At that moment, two burly corpses emerged out of nowhere, and seized the official just as he was loosening his pantaloons —

Which dropped to the floor, revealing a wrinkled manhood on which had been tattooed the word *mother,* topped with a turquoise merkin of phoenix feathers.

Éluma could not stop laughing.

But then she heard someone else laughing, too. Someone who stepped through a displacement field and stood across from her as viHurek struggled to free himself from the two servo-corpses.

"*Ori!*" She blurted out his child-name, an appalling breach of protocol, the se-cond one in as many minutes.

"I'll have you arrested," said Lang viHurek, "and then I'll rape the both of you."

"I'm afraid not," said Orifec. "We have signed a treaty with the High Council of Alykh, ratified by Inquestral sigil. This territory on which you stand remains Urna, and remains so until my family dies out, or otherwise relinquishes its right of fiefdom."

He held up a crystal globe on which were inscribed letters of fire in the High Scrript. Atop the globe was a sigil that anyone who had ever seen a street play would recognize — the mark of Ton Varushkadan el'Kalar Dath!

"You received an intervention from Mother Vara herself?" the official cried.

"The High Inquest does not make mistakes," said Orifec. "At least, none that they will admit to. But they are blessed with the High Compassion. And the House of Orifec, as a ruling house of a planet, can once in a while use the privilege of a tachyon bubble."

"You went to the High Inquest directly?"

"It's a card to be played

one time in a life, and I have had many, many lives without playing it."

"What was it like? How did the Inquestors seem? Were you struck by thunderbolts? Did their voices freeze your soul?"

"I'll tell you all about it, but first I want to go to the room that has no ceiling and no floor and boundaries ... where we can be one with the clouds and the rain.

***

Sajit waited.

Wandered, wondering at the scenes he saw, from niche to niche.

The holosculpts of the goddess were dedicated to the many joys of human coupling. There were images of contorted lovemaking, things that must physically be impossible, bends and twists and orifices Sajit did not know about, for the dead are infinitely malleable.

Sajit lapped at the *zul*-cone. Time passed, and he did not know whether to go next. Sometimes a suppliant would walk past, hand in hand with an acolyte or a servocorpse, perhaps on the way to a tryst.

As he waited, he suddenly felt Tijas.

Do you see pain?

He heard Arbát's voice. He felt Arbát's eyes staring, saw an unfathomable despair, and felt that very same despair in Tijas's mind ...

The only reason I exist is to save Sajit's life. This was the thought. *He and I are each other's death.*

He knew that this was why the doppling kit had been made and delivered to his home in Attembris. He knew, he had known almost since the beginning, yet he had not allowed himself to know what this really meant.

"Tijas," he whispered. Startled, an acolyte looked up and then returned to offering a votive lightshaft.

Somewhere back in the city, Arbát was peeling back the shell that protected Tijas's feelings. *I've been so selfish, not listening to him* Sajit thought.

How to console his twin, his brother, his other self.

Only the song he had heard as an infant....

Ýpna, kindekéh, ýpna enguestras din vezháh.... lundán-uraná

Sleep, child, sleep; The Inquestors are watching you from a far heaven....

He sang to himself, and softly, to send comfort to a distant soul through the aether of the mind, yet in the room the song echoed above the whispers....

***

... and Orifec and Éluma climaxed, as the warm rain lashed them, in the chamber where the cosmos curved in on itself and there was no beginning and no end.

Behind the subsiding thunder came the sound of a young boy's voice —

Ýpna, kindekéh, ýpna enguestras din vezháh.... lundán-uraná

Nestled in his arms, she turned to him. "That is how I imagine his voice now."

"Quiet, quiet, Éllekeh. This is not imagination. That *is* our boy. He is in this building somewhere."

With a subvocalized snarl she banished the room and they were in her inner sanctum, with the pool that reflected and the cool stone walls.

"Locate Sajit-without-a-Clan," Éluma said to the Temple's thinkhive.

Came the whisper of the thinkhive: *He is wandering through the Labyrinth, Goddess.*

"Lead him towards us," Éluma said,
***

Sajit found himself in a hallway, in a corridor, in a colonnade, in a cavern ... in quick succession ... with each step, the space changed shape ... but he did not feel lost. He clutched the ring in one hand, and as he walked he sang softly it was if the song itself was steering the thinkhive.

A garden. A forest. A wall. A castle. A rainbow. A stairway spiralling to nowhere. A horizon woven from rainbows and then the rainbows dissolved ... to a bright green field and a blue sky and distant trees with crimson leaves.

"Sajitteh...."

Orifec stood before him. And so did the woman. Both were cloaked in the same fabric of shadow, the one bolt of shadow stuff draped around them both.

Sajit said, "Father."

And Orifec did not deny it.

And to the goddess, Sajit said, "Mother."

He went to them and Éluma drew the cloak of shadow around all three of them. And Sajit felt the truth of their relationship, mind-to-mind, a tingling warmth.

Orifec spoke, but Sajit hardly listened. The words were just exposition; the joy was real.

Orifec said, "Listen. We have saved Urna for now. There will be a shield of force that separates us from Alykh, from the center of the palace of Nevéqilas around eighty klomets, and some villages will also be isolated and conjoined to Shírensang. We shall be an autonomous subworld, outside Alykh's jurisdiction ... and heritable by my descendants."

Éluma said, "Sajitteh, I've lived for this moment. I've lived for a time when we could be a family, like the ancients of Old Earth, living for each other." And she kissed him on the forehead. He felt the firmness of her love and yet ...

Sajit thought of Tijas, and once more felt his pain.

"Before we can become a family ..." Orifec said. "There is something I learned from Lady Varun-eh. Éluma, Sajit, the In-quest is coming. And you are listed for the culling."

"No!" Sajit said. "Not that, not now."

Orifec slipped from the cloak of shadow. He took Sajit by the hand. "You must not speak of him," he whispered, so Éluma would not hear. "She is a goddess. The values of Urna's society are fundamental to her. She wouldn't understand. She can't know about our plan ... to send the surrogate to the culling."

"It was not *our* plan!" Sajit grated. "You can't ever understand. We *are* each other, to lose him is to lose myself ... no one can under-stand this love I feel for him."

"You're wrong, Sajit. I *do* understand. I am the only person on this planet who understands."

He too kissed Sajit on the forehead. He dried Sajit's tears, and out of sympathy for Éluma, he tried to regain his composure.

But his heart screamed, *Tijas! Tijas!*

***

And beyond the force barrier, on the world that shared the same planet as this world, Tijas felt the scream. And wept bitterly, wept the tears that Sajit held back, wept alone in the crowded street, while their old tutor watched, uncomprehending.

Nine
Lady Varuneh

On a planet named Gallendys, an old woman waited in a small room. Her white hair was neatly bunned and she wore a sober and shapeless gray garment.

The room was at the point where twin cities met, each mirroring the other; Effelkang rising pyramidally from the ground, Kallendrang suspended pyramidally from the sky; where they met, a spherical room where every direction was down.

The woman was known as the Lady Varuneh, and she was awaiting the arrival of Gallendys's newly appointed Kingling, Ton Davaryush z'Gallendaran K'Ning.

Few in the twin cities of the towers of towers knew who Lady Varuneh really was, although there were worlds on which she was worshipped as a gooddess, or celebrated in epic poems. For the Lady Varuneh was not one to display her power. To most, she was just an old woman who had always been in service to the Kinglings of Gallendys.

Yet the signal for the arrival of a tachyon bubble was three standard days too early. Something, perhaps, had gone wrong. Lady Varuneh decided she had better confront whatever it was alone.

The bubble appeared and dissipated at once.

The man who stood there was unknown to her. "You're not the one I was waiting for," she said. It was a relatively young man; he had the demeanor of a ruler, but not the grooming of one.

"And this is not exactly what I expected, either," said the man. "I've activated my planet's *in extremis asistance* mode. The tachyon bubble that can only be used once in a dynasty, and which I am not allowed to control. So I must be where I am supposed to be. But I had expected — I don't know —"

"Perhaps a Grand Cabal of Inquestors, waiting around eon after eon to see which of the twenty thousand worlds needs urgent help?"

"No, mistress. I only thought —"

"That this room might be a little more dramatic-looking," said Lady Varuneh. "In any case, the *in extremis* rule means different things to different people."

"My dynasty has ruled for centuries," the young man said, "and I will be the last, so if I don't use the option, it will never have been used."

"Yours is a stable world, then," Varuneh listened for the whisper of the planetary thinkhive to give her the information she needed. "Urna, is it not?"

He bowed.

"And so you are the Princeling Orifec. An unusual planet, yours; half mired in superstition, half amongst the most civilized."

"I ask your help, mistress —"

"You do not recognize me."

Lady Varuneh did something she normally never did. She completely relaxed the muscles of her face, normally frozen in a mask of extreme old age. As he looked at her, he began to gasp —

***

The old woman was growing younger. The lines of age, deep furrows with dark shadows, were unchiselling themselves.

And at last the Princeling knew who had come to greet him, for he had seen her holosculpt in the innermost secret shrine of his ancestors.

"Mother Vara!" he cried out, prostrating himself, for this was more than a God, more, perhaps, even than an Inquestor.

"Once upon a time," she said. and her voice was remarkably gentle, though he knew she had seen the death and rebirth of man, "there was a world with a very long name ... it will come to me in a moment ...

a world called Brekison-eldylabruháh. There was a tremendous conflict on that world and there came a time when the ruling dynasty changed virtually every tennight, and virtually every tennight a new suppliant came to us. I hope your world is not like that."

"What happened to that planet, my Lady?"

"It *fell beyond* in a game of makrúgh," she said, rendering all its warring dynasties obsolete. "In its High Compassion, the Inquest thought obliteration was best; so the people of that world were not saved for another world. In a brief moment, painlessly, the world imploded. Pop!"

Orifec looked up and saw that the old woman's eyes were sparkling. "You're making a joke!"

"True," she said, "though it be in poor taste indeed. You'll forgive a twenty-thousand-year-old woman a senile moment from time to time."

Lady Varuneh summoned a chairfloat and stabilized the varigrav field so that the man would not be as disoriented. He started to speak again, but she held a finger to her lips.

"Traveling by tachyon bubble means that you are only moments from the place you left, and may return in moments. You have time. You may elect to return in the same moment that you arrived; so don't fret; we have time. Between tachyon journeys, it may be said that time stands still. Just as we ourselves say: *History there is, and no history.* Tell me of your life, Princeling."

Orifec blurted, "The High Inquest has made an error! Please find me a way to correct it!"

"The High Inquest doesn't make mistakes," Varuneh said. "Correcting one would not be appropriate." She seemed pensive. "There must be a way. Come, walk with me."

For a moment, she had a faraway look; Orifec saw that now the wrinkles were creeping back into her face. He realized now that she had done him an immense favor by showing him who she really was. He was trembling.

She took him by the hand. The walls deopaqued. She led him to a parapet and showed him the Sea of Tulangdaror. The wind was constant on the parapet, battering at his face, roaring. The sea sparkled. The woman stood on the parapet and the wind teased her hair so that it gradually undid its bun and began flying hither and thither. She looked old again, but he felt her youth as well; it was as if she were outside time itself.

Orifec felt the radiance of the High Compassion emanating from her eyes. He felt like a child. "I never believed I would ever lay eyes on —"

"I know. But you know, I have been in many places. Wherever I go, few ever realize I have been there until I am already gone."

"Mother Vara," Orifec said, "I humbly ask your help."

"Tell me, then," said Lady Varuneh, "for I have all the time you need. Start at the beginning."

***

Some megasleeps ago, Orifec told her, *before this body stands before you, this consciousness was in another soma....*

These things do not happen in time. They are in an eternal present, the entire sequence present as a single object, without directionality....

I am summoned from my bed. The moons are dancing. We are in the great glass garden at the heart of Nevéqilas and I am standing with my ten brothers and sisters, we are standing in a row, shortest to tallest. And my father, sitting on a gilded hover-throne, is watching us. And we are scared.

My father is a scary man.

We never see him, normally. We are reared by servocorpse-nannies. Each of us has one. They are programmed to love us with utter single-mindedness. We can do anything and they'll stop us from being hurt. We can run off a cliff and they'll run to stop us even though in pushing us back they will lose their footing and fall to their death — well, they are already dead anyway, so their death is no more death than their life is life.

My father says, Today is a big day. Today I choose my heir.

I love my father.

Behind each of us children stands a servocorpose with a cord of arachno-silk. The servocorpses have all been chosen for their strength. Their empathy circuits have been disabled; they are executioners.

My father says, I've loved all of you. *You, Adrina, the pretty one, who sings herself to sleep every night. You, Pontú, who loves to eat. You, Kiribáng, who enjoys hunting the phoenixes in the Forest of Kláh. You, Orifec, the quiet one. You....*

The names go on.

I say farewell to you all. I kiss you all. I have loved you.

With my last breath I will love and honour my father. He is good to me.

It is unfortunate that only one may succeed me. What I do now I do in love, so that there will be no fratricidal wars after my death.

I close my eyes and —

Feel the strangulating cord around my neck, hear the others as they struggle and gasp, but *I* feel ... no pain ... no lack of breath. Just the slender pressure of the silk.

Orifec, I choose you.

I open my eyes and the corpses of my brethren lie on the glass pebbles.

Let them be burnt, my father says, *for the flesh of princelings is to precious to be into feelingless servants.*

The ceremony: the central square of Shirénsang. The bodies of princelings laid on on a pyre woven from the branches of the fragrant flame-trees. And I am curled in foetal position inside a glass temperature-controlled egg, naked, vulnerable, a small boy who has just seen everyone he was close to murdered by the one he most loves.

The egg spins, suspended in a varigrav field above the fire that consumes princes. Inside the egg it is cool and the roar of the crowd is silenced. Time itself is askew, even the lips of the cheering crowd are moving in slow motion.

The flames leap up and envelop the egg and —

The egg cracks! I step forth and raise my palms in supplication to the ever-watchful eyes of the High Inquest.

I step forth, standing on a cube of force. With the movement of my hands comes the freezing of the flame. From fiery motion to icy stillness. The charred remains of my siblings now encased in cold pockets of liquid nitrogen. The bodies being moved by servo-corpses, piled pyramidally that I may step down to my world on the bodies of my brethren.

The steps are cold, so infinitely cold. As I stand naked at the top of the steps, the most highborn in the land ascend the steps and soon I am shod with pre-warmed fur boots, and wear a cape of translucent pearly clingfire. I am clad in a rainbow.

And a voice cries out over thousands of sound cubes that stud the columns of the square: *Behold the Princeling Orifec, who is to rule hereafter!*

Am I overwhelmed? Do I lose consciousness? There is a disjunction in the memory, for now I am in a room in the palace and I am with my father and I'm weeping, because he is dying.

Now I no longer fear him.

I fear myself.

Because the ritual is going to end with me killing my father. Thus it has been, thus it has always been. And this will go on, generation after generation. My father, my children, my father.

***

Arbát found Tijas weeping in the street. He had been aimlessly stumbling along the thin streets that threaded the newborn city. The emptiness he felt was indescribable. And when Tijas saw Arbát he wept even more, and Arbát held him, rocking him like a baby.

"There, there," he said. "The thing about pain is that eventually it ends. Or you become used to it, and that is the same thing."

Arbát wiped Tijas's tears with a corner of his robe. He took the boy by the hand and let him towards the nearest displacement plate.

"Where are we going?"

"To the old city," Arbát said. "To find somewhere to practice your exercises. Because if there's something can soften your pain, it's concentrating on your art."

Tijas thought, *But I can't tell you why I am in*

pain. *The thing that hurts is the thing I can never reveal.*

***

And the Princeling continued the recitation of his memories, while the Lady Varuneh listened solemnly, as they stood on the parapet that looked out on the Sea of Tulangdaror ... Yes, I see it clearly. An Inquestor has come in person to Nevéqilas. It's the Inquestor called Alkamathdes, whose title is the Supreme Hunter of U-topias.

I do not know how many generations ago this is. But I am Orifec. I am the same Orifec who saw my brothers and sisters killed so that I could inherit the throne. I haven't inherited yet, though. My father is still vigorous. This is not the scene where I am his bedside. I don't know. The scenes aren't linear.

My father says to the Inquestor, "It is such an honour you do us, *hokh'-Ton.*"

Ton Alkamathdes says, "We are here for the child-soldier culling, Prince-ling. But I chose to come in person because I have heard that you have an unusual ritual for determining the succession."

"It torments me," says my father.

"We have a suggestion."

He waves his hand in the air, creating a portable displacement field. In the circle there is a wooden box, not unlike a coffin. It is a gift. My father and I look at each other. Inquestors do not bring gifts, unless they come at a price impossible to pay. There is only one price: one's soul.

The Inquestor says, "This is ancient technology, older even than the Dispersal of Man. If you use it, you will never have to kill another child of yours. Except, of course, any children you have at the moment. You will also have to deny yourself any kind of love that could lead to the birth of a child. Or you will have to kill it."

My father says, "You mean, produce twins? Clones? But that is abomination!" He can hardly bring himself to utter the word.

"On some worlds," says the Inquestor. "But have you ever asked *why?*"

"Why would one ask? It's *harám*. They must be killed on sight. It's a basic tenet of the world."

"But why?"

And my father tells a story that he has known all his life....

***

When Urna was young, it was devoid of human life. Monsters lived in forests. Mounts were sharp-edged, not yet eroded into the gentle hills of now.

There were twin worlds in the system, closer to the sun, and each was the other's moon. They were called Ylas and Elas. They battled each other until both were close to annihilation. But Elas triumphed, at the cost of the destruction of all civilization in both worlds.

As their people were dying, as their technology was collapsing, a ship was launched which a microcosm of Ylas's culture. There were artists, philosophers, poets, and scientists, and they were led by the Princeling Áni, who was sired by a warrior king, Ánqit, and an In-questrix who had visited Ylas and abandoned her divine duties for the sake of love, she who was to be metamorphosed into the goddess Aërat.

The colony from Ylas, arriving in an empty world that with time was capable of great richness and plenty, multiplied. And presently there were born to a

Queen of the Ylians twins, Romú and Remú. And this was a wonder, because twins had not been seen among these people in hundreds of years.

The seers of the Ylians were horrified, and recommended that one be put to death. But the Queen demurred. She could not choose. She became distraught. At length, she carried them both in the forest, but weakened from labour, died on the way.

And so the boys grew in the wilderness, suckled by a feral pteratyger, imbibing animal habbits, not knowing human speech. But one day, borne on the pteratyger's back, they flew over the city that was called Naruvyilía, New Ylas, and they wanted to possess it.

They mustered an army of animals, who swooped down from the forest. The citizens were slain; one woman remained, the priestess of Aërat, who represented the living goddess, who was the most beautiful woman in the world, even before she had become the *only* woman in the world.

The woman spoke to them. Such was the sound of her voice that where they had been unruly, they grew calm. And she continued to speak to them, as she looked out from the portal of her temple, and she saw that all the people of the world were dead, and they saw her weeping. And they both desired her, even though the did not know what desire was, for they had known only each other, or the animals of the forest, and they had slaked their desires the only way they could, and that way was contrary to the laws of creation. She reached out with her two arms and with her left hand she touched the cheek of Remú and with her right the forehead of Romú. And when she touched them, speech entered their brains, for her mind was linked to the central thinkhive of the city.

Speech came all at once, like the light of a thousand stars. And suddenly they knew they had been dumb. And suddenly they knew they had been intemperate. And suddenly they knew they had been murderers.

In their fury — for they were mirror images of each other — they flew at each other, and at the goddess. They were simultaneously inflamed with lust and rage. They ripped at each other and made love to the goddess. The power of speech was bursting through them like a meteor shower.

They both entered the goddess at the same time. But Romú, who had entered from the rear, found resistance. It fired his anger and he slammed his fists into his twin's back with such force that he smashed bones and Remú fell dead.

Romú climaxed at the moment of his brother's death.

And the goddess turned to him, and she whispered, "Romú, Romú." And all at once, his rage left him.

He said, "We are all that is left. How shall we repopulate the world again?"

"Quiet," said the goddess. "We will fill this planet within seven generations; and all these dead will serve us."

And thus it was that servocorpses came to be in our world. But Romú would not allow his twin to serve. For he knew now that twins are an affront to the individual, to the separateness of each human from another. They blur the borders of identity.

And so it was that Remú's body was burned on a massive pyre, and since then there have never been any twins on Urna. One is always incinerated at birth. Without pain, of course. The choice is made by the thinkhive.

Except....

***

"You are royals," Ton Alkamathdes tells my father. "It is necessary that those who are raised up to rule must face more darkness than those who are not."

And my father accepts the gift of the doppling kit and its arcane technology. I am go be the last ruler to have different genes from my successor.

When the ruler tires, or is too ill to go on, his memories pass to the one in the doppling kit, whose first duty is to devive the previous Princeling. Since that visit from Hokh'Ton Ton Alkamathdes, it has been this way.

And since then our world has flourished. We are few but we are prosperous. Urna is a backwater but it is a world with a single beautiful city and numerous villages where people live simple and idyllic lives.

Until another world disgorged itself on top of ours.

***

Lady Varuneh listened to the tale the Princeling spun.

She said, "The universe, and our place in it, is precariously balanced. A tiny shift can bring down an entire world. Come with me. You still have time."

The Lady Varuneh summoned a skiff with two chairfloats. There was no upper platform. They were to travel as equals.

She closed her eyes, subvocalizing directions to the skiff's thinkhive. The skiff whirred, soared, and soon was flying over Tulangdaror. At the moment the sea was mirror-still. It glittered with the reflected light of Gallendys's suns. Rainbows lanced the yellow sky. All along the shore, there ran an elevated river.

"Do you see this river?" she told him. "It's a river of liquid nitrogen and it leads straight to the starship factories, without which our galaxy-spanning civilization would be lost."

Orifec watched. The river followed the outline of the shore, then angled abruptly off to the right.

Do you see them, floating in the river?

Orifec saw vast creatures floating down the cold river, creatures that seemed to be almost all brain. No eyes, no other visible organs of perception, but with a cetacean shape.

"They are *setálikas,*" said Lady Varuneh, "delphinoids. They are journeying towards our shipyards where they will be soldered, still living, into the hulls of our ships."

And now they were crossing a desert named Zhnefftikak. A forbidding terrain. Outcrops with twisted tines.

Rearing up ahead there was a mountain. But what a mountain! It was so tall that it appeared to slice the sky in two. It was the mountain's shadow that formed the wasteland of Zhnefftikak.

"Skywall," Lady Varuneh said, "that's what the locals call it."

As they went closer, the dark wall filled their field of vision. It eclipsed the suns. They were in a deeper darkness than any darkweaving.

"Let's go closer." Varuneh said, and Orifec felt a cold as well. Varuneh had the skiff illuminate the wall and now as they climbed a small circle of radiance rose with them, illuminated the wall which was featureless. "This mountain was created during eons ago in the planet's past, when it had a denser atmosphere. Inside, it's hollow. Within is the place called Keian zenz-Atheren, the Sunless Sound. And there is a howling, whirling and utterly dark wind inside it, and in that wind dwell the wind-bringers. They sing, but not music; they sing with light, this delphinoids, as they plough through the thick darkness. The light they produce is the same light as the light-mad overcosm, but it is not chaos; it is chaos con-strained into concord, for the delphinoids see the myriad connections throughout the overcosm; they see what our astrogators need to see, to open up the pathways within the overcosm along which our ships can travel. This you must know. Inside the mountain are a people that we created, who hunt the delphinoids and deliver them to a cavern where they are transported via displacement plates to the Cold River.

"The people inside the mountain do not know of us, do not know why they harvest the delphinoids, do not know of space travel; most of all, they do not know of the light songs, for we created them deaf and dumb. Otherwise they would go mad. This music of sound and color affects normal people that way.

"Yet the entire culture is a construct, dreamed up by a thinkhive, every myth and tradition carefully manufactured so these people will do what they must do. And because of this artificial creation, this *lie* if you will, our ships sail the overcosm. And if the delphinoid hunters one day should learn that there is another world beyond the mountain ... what should happen then?"

The skiff came to a ledge. All was perfectly black, but the Lady Varuneh subvocalized a command and a part of the wall dissolved, allowing them to enter.

"There is a small chamber here. You may enter it, but you may not remain for longer than a few seconds, or you will go mad." She motioned for Orifec to enter an inner door.

Orifec went in by himself. There was a seat, more a cushion of force that softened to accommodate him.

All at once, the walls dissolved, and he was in the midst of the delphinoids' lightsong.

It was light of every color, blending, blurring, whirling, unfurling, streaming, soaring, plum-meting, cascading — and the sounds! — whistling, droning, screeching, thundering, sussurating, percussive, lyric, all at once. And the emotions: wrenching, seductive, despairing, elated, but over-riding all else a pefect blend of grief and joy.

In the song of the delphinoids Orifec relived his life and the lives all all the past Orifecs, the lives all intertwisting and intertwining, knotting and unknotting, warping and woofing into ever-shifting tapestries — and Orifec wept, wept like a child, because of the beauty, the indescribably longing ...

All this in but a few seconds, because the walls reopaqued, and suddenly he was alone, and in silence, and in darkness.

And he was left with an ache that would never go away. A sense of loss. A grief.

"Let us go back to the twin cities," Varuneh said. He heard her as though coming from another world.

***

The Lady Varuneh was silent for a time. "I do not know why I showed you the secret of Skywall Mountain," she told him.

But there was more; on the way back to Effelkang and Kallendrang, she also told him of the web dancers.

"Each delphinoid ship-mind used a focusing-crystal that comes from a mountain on a very different, very distant planet," she told him as they rode the wind, "a planet without even a name. The crystals are teased from caverns deep within the mountains by web dancers, children of the Clan of Rax, whose dance is a sexual teasing — for the mountains are living, and the crystals are their eggs. There was a time when only one web dancer remained in all of the Dispersal of Man, and our entire universe hung upon the intricacies of a single dance."

What was she trying to tell him? That huge, galaxy-shaking events often came down to the actions of a single person? That everything they knew could be destroyed in an instant by one event on a planet that didn't even have a name?

After that they were silent all the way to the small room at the juncture of the two cities. Orifec knew that she was showing him unusual favor. He also knew that she would take her time before revealing the full nature of that favor.

Fnally when they were once more in the chamber, Varuneh said to him, "I am an Inquestor, and you know that we hunt utopias. We are enemies of the static, the unchanging, and for that reason we may cause worlds to *fall beyond.*

When Ton Alkamathdes brought you the doppling kit, it was because your planet was trapped in a recursive cycle of fratricide. Ending the cycle made your world, in its own small way, a utopia. And thus it is, Princeling, that in finding love, in making yourself a family, you too have hunted a utopia in your own way. You have made an end that is a beginning. And for that, I will help you."

The Princeling knelt before the Inquestrix. He touched her feet with his palms. She said to him, "Here, I will give you the treaty you request, sealed with the sigil of the High Inquest. And in return ... you shall make love to me. I am several centuries old, and now and then, I desire the touch of someone younger."

And she kissed him.

And in its own way that kiss was as transformative as the seconds he had spent immersed in the Light on the Sound.

For he had been kissed by the mother of all mankind.

***

**NEXT ISSUE
BOOK THREE:**

***COLLECTORS
OF CHILDREN***

Professor Schnau-en-Jip

Frequently Asked Questions about the Inquestral Highspeech

Why are High Inquestral verbs so complicated?

Bhasháhokh, the Inquestral Highspeech, has a uniquely complex verb system. Part of this is the old Indo-European system of passive and active, singular, dual and plural, aorist, perfective and imperfective ... already splitting a single word into dozens of forms and lists of endings.

But part of it is more complex than that. High Inquestral ceased to be spoken as a native language about twenty thousand years before the earliest events described in the Inquestor novels. In its heyday as a literary and poetic language, it was therefore not used in regular discourse. Even the Inquestors did not speak High Inquestral all the time; the language was used in games of *markrúgh,* or in the most elevated forms of literature. It was expected to be difficult to understand.

What evolved was that many alternate forms, subtle differentiations of meaning expressed by inflection, came into use. Many variant was of expressing the same tense evolved as well in order to fit the exigencies of poetic prosody.

From the morphological point of view, there are basically two types of verb: *weak* and *strong*. Strong verbs have two stems which need to be learned separately, mostly involving a vowel change, and take *-un* as a past participle ending. Weak verbs have no umlautization of the stem and have part participles ending in *-et*.

Intransitive verbs denoting mental states *may* optionally be conjugated deponently, i.e. in the passive voice but with active meaning. This is a survival of a more archaic middle voice.

The basic forms available for regular verbs are:
ACTIVE: IMPERFECTIVE ASPECT
Present, future, imperfect
AORIST
Past Historic
PERFECTIVE ASPECT
Present perfect, pluperfect, future perfect
SUBJUNCTIVE
imperfective, perfective
PASSIVE: IMPERFECTIVE ASPECT
Present, imperfect, future
AORIST
Past Historic
PERFECTIVE ASPECT
Perfect, pluperfect, future perfect
SUBJUNCTIVE
imperfective, perfective
IMPERATIVE

Two other series of tenses are available for most verbs, based on the CAUSATIVE STEM which is created by reduplication of onesyllable roots with umlautization in both monosyllabic and polysyllabic roots and an extra *e-* prefixed for monosyllables beginning with a vowel:

shãtro I sing *sheshãitrái* I cause to sing
aíro I love *eayrái* I cause to love
perpálo I juggle *perpailái* I juggle

Not all tenses are available in the causative stem. The original usage of this stem was to form *synthetic perfect tenses* using the imperfect and aorist suffixes, but in the dialect of Varezhdur, which is considered standard, these tenses are formed analytically. Used with the subjunctive active endings, the causative mood is created:

dávekin sheshãitráis You cause the boy to sing

The object of causation is generally in the dative case. When it is in the locative case, the verb acquires a passive meaning.

Essondrá eayráis You cause Essondras to be loved

When used with the subjunctive *passive* endings, the meaning is medio-passive:

Sheshãitreúreste You have been singing for yourself

Occasionally the reduplicated stem is not clearly visible as reduplicated and the post-enclitic *-ke* is optionally added for clarity. This particle can combine with a preceding *m*, *˜*, or *t*, *th*, *d*, to form *enke*, *-nke*, or *-kke*.

The final available series is based on the DESIDERATIVE stem, which is characterized by sigmatization of the main stem, often with sandhi, and the second umlaut of the main vowel. These forms are often irregular and sometimes created "on the fly" especially in poetry *shãtro* becomes *shẽsso* or *shensho:*

When preceded by the particle *shá,* we derive the primary desiderative meaning:

shá shẽsso   I wish I could sing

Only the present and aorist endings are available in this usage, and they are used to express aspect only, not tense.

When *shá* is used with the subjunctive, the meaning is desire on the part of the subject for an action by aother (in the ablative case).

shá shẽssaeis   It is desired that you both sing
sha Enguesti plassái I am desired to weep by the
                        Inquestor, i.e. the Inquestor
                        wants me to weep.

This form can be used for extremely polite requests, but also for an ironically polite command. When *shá* is followed by a vowel, it is normally elided.

This introduction to the complexities of the High Inquestral verb will be continued in the next issue of *Inquestor Tales.*

Never published cover for Asimov's Magazine for *The Dust,* by Karl Kofoed; owing to a top-down redesign of the magazine, this gorgeous cover was never used

LOST TALES

The Dust

The dust came first: dormant, unstirring, hugging the hard crust of Aëroësh for an eon or more. The tempests that had ground it out of the stone were forgotten; now, weather-shifts later, the winds were stilled and the heat stifling and rasp-dry. Time-frozen, blood-dyed by the red sun that Aëroësh. circled, the dust ocean stretched from eyes' end to eyes' end, crimsoning with distance and melting into brown-red sky.
From the earliest times the thinkhives of the Dispersal of Man had known of Aëroësh, but had deemed it too distant and too inhospitable for Man... .
In time came disturbances, tugging at the power of the Inquest. The Inquestors moved planets to make room for a war. And the people bins went out, towed by convoys of delphinoid shipminds that pinholed through the overcosm beyond real-space, each one of them stasis-stacked with the survivors of murdered worlds; for in its com-passion the Inquest was compelled to save what people it could. And so men came to —

Aëroësh: scavengers, dispossessed, clanless, despairing. Their cities sprang up from the rockface under the dust, domed with forceshields, linked by klomets of burrow-tubes. They were fragile bubbles of humanity, buried in the soundless depths of the dust-dead sea.
And then Aëroësh changed. Surges of power erupted from the cities. The dust rippled. The forceshields hummed. The ion wind came, and the dust woke at last, in slow spiralling storms a thousand klomets broad, gusting, sweeping the plains, like an

army without a foe. There were no mountains to scour, no people to eat alive. The storms were impotent.
And the people of Aëroësh were untouched by them. They lived far down, in the cities with skies of dust. At times they forgot that the rest of the human race existed. In turn, they were ignored. The Inquestor who ruled Aëroësh held sway over a dozen worlds; he never came. There were no visi-tors ... for what did the planet have but dust? And who could love the dust?
The dust waited, gusting in darkness and light.

***

The palace! A dance of golden spirals and glitter-burnished spires, easing into orbit around Alykh, the pleasure world. And there in the throne room tiled with azurite and ringed with columns of cold blue flame, the Princeling Elloran, Inquestor, Hunter of Utopias, and Lord of Varezhdur and all its Tributaries, watching the crescent of Alykh burning in the blackness and listening to the cool music: flutes, watergongs, whisperlyres, shimmerviols.
He too was watched. Shen Sajit, master of the Prince's music, reclining against the curvewall of the sunken orchestra pit, was not bothering to hear his own composition, heard a hundred times already.
With a clap the Inquestor summoned Sajit. Sajit approached him, sunken in his throne with his shimmercloak strewn over the gold steps patterned with a sequent frieze of quartz-eyed pteratygers.
The music went on, not needing direction.
"You seem so tired, so remote," said Sajit. He could talk so directly because when they were boys he had saved Ton Elloran's life.
"Wouldn't you be? We'-ve just come from another war."

"Yes. You commanded the migrations of a dozen people bins. Very tiring work. Yet you showed no emotion at all." Try as he might, he could not conceal the irony in his voice. For a moment he remembered —

Chasing the people bins into the overcosm, the, slow dance of the black ships against the glittering firelights of the space between spaces, and then the last people bin vanishing like a dust-mote drifting from light into shadow ... and a single tear on the Prince's cheek.

Sajit remembered thinking: Perhaps he is human. How should I know? We are the same age, and yet his face is far more youthful than mine, except for those gray eyes radiating all the ancientness of the Inquest's power. As well befriend the mountains or the stars, he had thought, cautioning himself against feeling too much involvement with the Inquestor.

"Look at it," Elloran said, interrupting Sajit's reverie. "Alykh, the pleasure world—"

"Where we'll go down to Airang, city of cheap love," said Sajit, "and we'll ride the varigrav coasters and drink sweet zul and dance in the gem-paved streets, until —"

"Until we have forgotten all our pain."

We'll be *dorezdas*, thought Sajit. And Ton Elloran will never see the Sewer Labyrinth or the husks of dead palaces where live the thieves and the beggars and the ugly and the dying, those who call Alykh their homeworld, who eke out an existence by fleecing the dorezdas with their eyes on the stars and their minds on the problems of the rich and their pockets lined with arjents. But I will know. Could it really have been twenty years since a filthy, bone-thin boy had fled the city, clinging to the tunic of a broken old wandering dreamsinger?

"You were born here, weren't you, Sajit?"

Aírang. Home. "Yes. But now I'm a dorezda with fine clothes and a clan-name and a place at an Inquestor's court — " He remembered home as a hovel in the mbble and he turned his mind to music, trying to forget.

Lazily the railinged floater fell towards the city. Ton Elloran standing apart from the others, alone even amid his dozen attendants. A delicate fang scented vapor gauzed them.

You're burying your pain, aren't you? Sajit thought. Burying deep inside yourself the memory of the war.

From a corner of the floater, a quartet of whisperlyres played and a boy singer sang softly of a lost love he could never have known; for Ton Elloran never went anywhere without his own music, he could not bear the silence. Below them, the city —

Aírang of the dorezdas! Pillars of klomet-high varigrav coasters, etch-veined Ontian marble knuckle-dust-studded with amethysts, darkstriping the purple sunset ... jousting giant reptiles clawing the sunlight and pawing a screechy thunderdust over tiers of cheerers ... Aírang of the tower-tall buildings warpwoofed with jewel-threads of streets and echo-rich with laughter...

They reached the guesthostel of Ton Exkandar, Kingling of the Alykh system, a high tower of brick and vine, wound round with a spiral balcony. As the floater eased on to the dais that jutted from the topmost turret, Sajit spoke to Elloran.

"Let me alone into the city awhile, Inquestor."

Ton Elloran turned. "But Sajit, my music — "

"This is my homeworld." But as he said it it rang false.

"Of course. It must have been twenty years." Elloran paused to straighten his shimmercloak, which glowed faint pink against the dark blue fur. "Of course you must go, Shen Sajit." And then, "Will you let me come with you? Will you show me what this city really is?"

"You don't want to know."

"I'm tired of wearing my mask of compassion," Elloran said. "I've pried a trillion people loose from their worlds like so many barnacles ... I'm losing touch, Sajit!"

"Yes."

The floater now was still, and the sounds of the city assailed them: hawkers' shouts, the strumming of distant dreamharps, the whoosh of the rich men's gaudy floaters — some mere circles of metal that wove their way through the forest of towers, some with great caparisons of peacocks' wing and gilt, sailing majestic through the violet sky, some with crimson-cloaked trumpeters sounding brash sennets ... Sajit waved to an attendant, dissolved the darklfield that englobed the Inquestral floater. Seeing the glitter of the shimmer-cloak, a man cried out and the traffic jam of floaters parted suddenly. A ray of mauve-dyed sunset fell on the square below the parapet; people wriggled like little worms. A gate irised in the turret to admit Elloran's party. As Elloran stepped in he tore the shimmercloak from his body. ...

One did not understand Inquestors, Sajit thought as they drifted slowly down the airtube to the surface of Alykh. He glanced at his own clothes — the short cloak of cloth-of-iridium trimmed with dingfire, the kaleidokilt of the clan of Shen with its semisentient buckle of two mating flamefish — and thought: I've become one of the very things I used to despise, the people whose pockets I picked and whomI used to beg from... .

And beside him Elloran floated, frozen-faced. Others fell above and below, streaking the mirror metal of the air shaft. What does he know? Sajit thought bitterly. He remembered the burning planets and the people packed in their people bins, and the Inquestor's impassive, soft-spoken com-mands. He's blown Up pla-nets, but he hasn't stood at the gateway of the Sewer Labyrinth and smelt the stink of the dead ... and he pitied Elloran then. He must always be alone, after all, and have slaves for friends and feel compassion instead of love and play the Inquestral game of makrúgh instead of living relationships.

At the floor of the shaft, about to step into the street, he thought: Perhaps I should show him those things. The windstream ruffled his hair and he pulled his cloak tighter. Sunset came swiftly on Alykh, and he knew it would be night now, a night more garish-gaudy even than the day. "Here," he said, "you don't want to be without your music." He pulled a songjewel from a fold in his kilt, snapped it awake, and placed it around his master's neck. It was a quartet of shimmer-viols, and Elloran smiled a little. A door dissolved; Aírang's noise assaulted them. Sajit stepped on to the street and turned to Elloran with a twisted smile. "My home," he said, with an ironic sweep of the hand.

He led the Inquestor through a glass-cobbled square where revellers skied the bright night sky on threads that were yoked to pteratygers, their pink feathered wings flapping as they soared and wheeled... .

"Where are we going?" Elloran said.

"I'll show you," Sajit snap-ped, ignoring court protocol. But Elloran did not seem to notice.

"Artists," he muttered, and Sajit felt a ghost of their old friendship for a second. They found a displacement plate at the comer of the square and Sajit leapt on to it, not waiting for his master.

... They stepped through a corridor of an indoor

theater, masked actors moving solemnly to a slow heartbeat of a drum and singsonging in piercing artificial voices, dead husks of men perhaps, animated by hidden thinkhives to imitate the dead classics, and the audience murmuring in languid unison... .

"Come!" said Sajit urgently. Elloran followed behind, not observing that the servant had taken the lead. For a moment Sajit thought. I'm pushing too much, he's always allowed me to speak freely but he's not my friend, he's an Inquestor ... but recklessness seized him.

... an orgy-field drenched in fang vapors, the field itself thrumming softly to the rhythm of a hundred lovers ... a shrill street opera ... a slave market ... the varigrav coasters looming high in the distance, with specks of people as they plummeted on antigraviton fields, swarm-ing like fireflies... .

And then darkness.

And silence, save for a whisperbuzz of shimmerviols from the Inquestor's song-jewel. "Are you afraid?" said Sajit. There was a stale breeze in the darkness, tainted with a tang of death.

"No."

"Do you want to see where I grew up?"

Elloran didn't answer.

"This is the Sewer Labyrinth," Sajit said, "that runs beneath the city. We used to play here. Come on."

They passed through twisted tunnels, and Sajit, growing used to the darkness — there was a faint phosphorescence here — saw Elloran watching everything, memorizing everything ... the stagnant canals, the old bones, an old man with gouge-yellow cheeks, staring listlessly from behind a frayed wisp of blanket, the children who ran after them throwing stones and jeering... .

"I was one of those," Sajit said. They emerged into a street, barely man-wide, a displacement plate that didn't work, buildings strung together from sheet metal and old starship hulls. Striding fiercely through the garbage, Sajit made for his old hovel, knowing that it could no longer be there, that buildings sprouted and withered overnight here in the slums of Aírang. "I would have died here if I weren't a survivor."

They threaded their way through endless reeking alleyways, and Sajit realized he would never find his old home. He was angry, and he wanted to be cruel.

Above them the sky glowed, now fluorescent green, now garish pink ... the lights of Aírang were all that the hovel city needed. They reached Rats' Valley, hemmed in by two hills of refuse, nick named for the rodents that scurried pitter-patter through the dark and preyed on the babies, dead or discarded, half-buried in the rust and dust.

They stopped. A cloud of dust made Sajit cough.

Finally Elloran said, "What do you want of me, Sajit?"

"Powers of powers, Inquestor! I just want you to admit you're human too, I just want you to step down from your mountain of power and touch the people you kill by the billions ... look!" He kicked up a flurry of dust and dried excrement. "I was bom out of this dust, Elloran! And you came out of a Prince's palace. Yet you destroy planets, and I make songs." He turned away. He had broken all the bounds of propriety. In public it would have been certain death.

"You too, Sajit," Elloran said at last. To Sajit's annoyance he did not seem angry. "There are times when I think you almost understand, but ..." He tore the songjewel from his throat and flung it into the debris. A single clank and it was gone. "Are you satisfied now?"

"You asked to be punished. Ton Elloran."

"Yes. Yes." The Inquestor turned back and began walking back to the slum and the Sewer Labyrinth. Was he angry? Sajit could not read him. Perhaps they had quarrelled, if a person could be said to have had a quarrel with an Inquestor. Sajit let him go. He didn't know whether he had made his point or not. He was tired and he wanted a woman. Why not? he thought. I'm a dorezda now. With a flick of his mind he turned on the tracer at his wrist so that Elloran could find him if he needed him. Perfunctorily he flicked the dust from his clothes a little, and then he headed towards the whores' quarter. The stinking streets went by in a blur, and when he reached the first of the operational displacement plates the squares of the city went by, their colors jangling dissonances... .

"Master, master ..." a wheezing voice. Sajit turned. Standing by a pillar of flame, the old man beckoned him. The face was indecently withered; he had probably let it age in the old way as a grotesque tourist attraction. "You want a girl?" Sajit didn't answer, and the old man came closer, bowing himself in two. "I have such girls, master, such girls, and for a mere demiaijent they will lull you with song and yield to your masterly touch ... you do not speak, master! Is it boys you favor? I have such boys also ... do you want pain and punishment, do you want strange alien creatures perhaps? I—"

"*De zon dorezda!*" Sajit snapped in the local lowspeech.

"You are no *dorezda!*" the man said, not switching to the lowspeech. "I see you have learnt some of our words, excellency. You come here often then ... for one of such discernment as you, I have other things ... lo ..." He snapped his fingers and summoned holosculpt miniatures out of the thin air. Women wheeled and dissolved into other women, and all had the perfect body and the perfect face that marked the Alykhish pleasure girl, the bodies rebuilt each year before they became too worn ... "But sir," said the pimp, "I see you are interested, and yet you don't speak. Don't be embarrassed, master! Perhaps in your palace you dare not speak your desire, from modesty or from compassion, but here there is nothing one dare not desire, nothing your demi-aijent will not buy ... of course," his voice fell to a sly whisper, "there is a surcharge for death."

"Powers of powers!" Sajit cried, "I speak my mother's tongue and you flatter me for picking up a few foreign phrases! I come looking for a woman and you show me images of my mother!"

"I see," said the old man, uneasy now. "You are a child of Airang. Well, I have just the thing. Follow."

Sajit felt a surge of anger. For such a one as this his mother must have worked, despising the *dorezda* who spawned him.

Shrugging, he followed the old man as he hobbled towards the fiery pillar. The pillar parted and they stepped into a cool atrium. Above their heads was a still holosculpt caelorama of a cloudless bloodred sky. The floor of the atrium was dust.

And in the center of the atrium, in a startling shaft of white light, a slow nebula of dust swirled... .

"She is not a mere whore-without-a-clan, excellency," the old man was buzzing. Sajit ignored"him, entranced by the strange dust-sculpture. He had seen such things before, but never so classical , . . it was like one of the ancient songs, strophic, pentatonic, nothing to it at all. All the events of the day seemed senseless beside this... .

"It's unbelievable," he said, "Who could have done such a thing? From which

Inquestral court does it come?"

"He said I was no clanless whore, dorezda." A woman had stepped out from behind the dust sculpture. Sajit noticed at once the beige hair streaked with turquoise, streaming behind her because of the field that held the dust sculpture in place. The hair was the only luxury; she wore a rough brown smock, as though she had stepped right out of the Sewer Labyrinth, and her face must have been unrefurbished for at least two years; it even sagged in places. "I am Dei Zhendra of the clan of imagers, a dust sculptress."

"Is she not beautiful, master, is she not as classic as the ancients were, before our cosmetics and our artificial faces, eh?" said the pimp, nudging Sajit suggestively in the ribs.

"Get out!" Sajit cried. He whirled around and the man was gone. Somewhere outside a beggar boy was singing. "You shouldn't be doing this!" Sajit said. "How can you demean yourself so much, Zhendra?" The woman was beautiful; not as the pleasure girls were beautiful, but beautiful also because of what she had done.

"Dust is expensive, excellency." There was a bitter mocking in her voice. She led him behind the dust nebula and he saw sacks of dust piled neatly against the far wall. "Not every kind of dust will do, you know. At your feet is the common dust, a gipfer a sack, useless, useless, useless. It will not bear the static charge you need for this." She pointed to the sculpture. As it swirled, motes sparkled and died. "You see, the best dust comes from the other end of the Dispersal of Man. From a planet called Aëroësh."

"Aëroësh ... in an old dead tongue, 'the dust'."

"It is a beautiful dust. A dust on tiny silicate chains, charged and polarized, that reach for each other and flow and swirl almost like a living thing... ."

"You've found no sponsor, Dei Zhendra?"

She laughed, then, a terrible, despairing laugh. "Who can love the dust?" she said. "Three sacks I bought last year for five hundred aijents, and the pimp takes eighty percent... ." And then she said, "And I would rather sell my body than be a slave to a Princeling's whim, dust-sculpting the likenesses of his mistresses and having no square of earth to call my own."

"But you're wrong!" said Sajit heatedly, even as he was drawn to the woman, seeing deep inside her an echo of himself.

She laughed again. "What do you care? You won't see me again after tonight. I never have a man twice. So tell me how you want it and stop searching my soul. Excellency."

"Zhendra — " he reached out for her but he couldn't feel any sexual passion. He knew he wanted to get her out of there, he wanted to show her how much they were kin to each other, how they had both striven to reach above the garbage heaps and embrace the whole Dispersal of Man, but —

"Here," she said, mocking again. She was lying down in the dust and stripping off her smock, and then she flung it aside so casually, so gracefully. Even here she was all artist, not needing the makeup and the facelifts at all.

"In the dust?"

She only laughed. He felt aroused at last, and knelt down to kiss her.

They heard footsteps. Sajit jumped up in a panic. The dust flew wildly for a moment... .

"I am sorry, Sajit." Elloran stepped into the room, his shimmer cloak churning up the dust. "I don't know why I eavesdropped on your tracer, why I came here... ."

The woman had risen now. Sajit bit his tongue.

He could not show his anger here, in front of a strange woman; one knew better than to intrude on an Inquestor's dignity.

But Zhendra shrieked, "Get out."

Elloran walked slowly around the dust-sculpture. Then he looked long and still at the woman, shaming her to silence at last. But she did not beg his pardon. Elloran smiled the wan little smile he often had that was meant only for Sajit. Sajit struggled to contain himself. If he had not known how compassionate an Inquestor must always be, he would have sworn that Elloran was trying to hurt him deliberately.

"You have taste, Sajit," Elloran said. "She is beautiful." Could he actually be trying to take her away from him? Then he said, "I at least am not a slave, eh, Sajit? Not to any man. Only to the whole Dispersal, only to mankind itself. Oh, you should pity me ... would you like a palace of your own, girl, and a sack of dust a day?"

He's drugged! Sajit realized at last. He's let himself lose control—

How could an Inquestor say these things?

"Well?" Elloran shouted. "Shall I drag you away from this creature who reminds you so much of your lowly origins? Would you like a planet of your own? I have a dozen! I have Ymvyrsh, I have Eldereldad, I have Menjifarn, Kailasa, Chembrith, Muralgash, Gom, Aëroësh —"

He saw Zhendra's eyes widen, star-sapphire-blue, heard her little gasp

He didn't want to look at them. She was using the Inquestor! And the Inquestor was using her to get back at him! It smacked of makrúgh, the complex game of power that only Inquestors played ... and yet he knew that Elloran could not be playing *makrúgh*. You didn't play *makrúgh* with an underling. He wheeled around until he faced the whirling nebula.

The dust twisted slowly, sparks shifting from shining to shadow.

You've won, Elloran, he thought resentfully.

Varezhdur the golden palace circled the pleasure planet until the days of the Cold Season trickled away. It did not grow warmer or colder, of course; the names of the seasons were legacies of a lost past. The palace grew too: a wing for the woman of dust, a maze of chambers twistier than a conch-shell's innards, a forcedome outside the walls where a nebula of dust grew daily beneath the starstream that it echoed.

Hour after hour Elloran would watch her. On the mirror metal floor lay countless strands of dust, formed and charged and ready to be activated into the pattern with a deft wrist-flick. Prom a recess in the floor Sajit's music would play. His music was harsher now. No more the shimmerviols and the whisperlyres, but the clang of kenongs and klingels and glass-shatterers beneath shrill highwoods. Zhendra labored, scooping up armfuls of the charged dust and flinging them into the field, sometimes diving into the cloud to draw out swirls of dust with her charger, sometimes deactivating a whorl so that its motes fluttered to the floor. She did not notice the music; she did not seem to notice the Inquestor either. Away from the dust she seemed only half alive; enveloped in it, dancing in the dust, she seemed to become part of it, to become a single, breathing organism with it. Sajit envied her her freedom. He knew that even when she slept with the Inquestor she could not feel like his possession.

As the Cold Season ended she came instead to him, seeking variety perhaps. Sometimes he would know that she had just come from Elloran, but she never said anything. He didn't question his good fortune. Her lovemaking was violent; always she wanted to lead the way. Their bodies were flaming and yet he would always know that her mind was far away. He felt like a dustmote that had veered too near the sun. Perhaps he was in love.

In the Season of Mists the palace moved into orbit around Kailasa. In small floaters they would chase the sunlight, skimming the clouds, pausing to hunt the fierce lighthawks with their ten-meter wings leaf-bright with chlorophyll as they grazed off the brilliant sunlight; or to trap the firephoenixes as they mated, shrieking, in mid-air. When they tired they would change direction and follow the night, playing zigzag races through the rifts in the Mountains of Jérrelahf. And when they tired of that too they swung south and rode the flying sea-serpents in the Pallid Ocean and harvested the honey-eggs that floated on the waves cracking them open to quench their thirst. Or north to ski on snow-slopes dyed scarlet by hardy bloodalgae. Always the Inquestor would ride, alone but for the music and the master of music, and Sajit always played the new harsh music, not wanting to give his master the sorrow-drowning sweetness that he craved. Since that evening not long after the last war when they had both found Zhendra, Elloran had not lost control of himself. He had not said a word when Zhendra began visiting both of them, for an Inquestor could not hang on to material things. Sajit knew that Elloran was hurt. He had to be. Unless Inquestors really were like automated thinkhives and not like human beings... .

Admit your hurt! he would think silently, whipping up the musicians to a maenad frenzy. But Elloran would stand and watch his courtiers cavorting and sometimes he would even smile.

And after, when they were too tired even to float

and watch the circling of lighthawks or phosphor-leafed forests quivering in the double moonlight, they would leave this unpopulated world and go back to Varezhdur to do what had been obsessing their thoughts all the while... .

The nebula had grown to the height of three men; twice the force-dome had been expanded. The dust had come from Aëroësh at staggering expense, by tachyon bubble. An extravagance only an Inquestor could command, for it was said that whole suns died to fuel those specks of realspace that flashed instantly from world to world, bypassing even the overcosm of the delphinoid shipminds. The gesture had maddened Sajit even as he wanted her to get her dust in time.

She worked and Elloran watched her, both oblivious of the increasing dissonance. Angrily Sajit clapped his hands for silence. "Will it never be done?" he shouted. Zhendra worked on. But Elloran whirled and cried out, "It must never be finished! I never want her to finish it!"

For they both knew what she would do when the nebula was done.

Ton Elloran was a consummate player of *makrúgh*, the game of war and power that pitted Inquestor against Inquestor. With that single war he had deflected the wars of the Dispersal away from his own sector, with only a planet or two destroyed; now they could expect peace for a few years.

The Mist Season became the Season of Rains. The palace Varezhdur came to Chembrith, the chief world of Elloran's principality. Two whole continents were covered with the thinkhives that coordinated the worlds Elloran ruled. Another continent housed the starships sent from far Gallendys. And the fourth contained the cities; Angesang with its twisting walls you could see even from space, writhing like copulating snakes; Tathenthrang with its rainbow-tiered terraces, hanging over the Lake of Octagons; Ghakh of the thousand pyramids, with its university; Dhandhesht where were stored the holoramic memories of dead worlds. Solitude turned to the business of government. Diplomatic receptions on floatislands hovering over the Lake, where spectacles of times before the Dispersal were enacted over the waters to the strains of thousand-man orchestras. Fierce games of *makrúgh* played over interstellar distances, convocations of Inquestors, stiff and stemfaced in their shimmercloaks, sipping zul in small palace chambers. New programs for the thinkhives to mull over.

For Sajit there was new music to write; every event, every new inning of *makrúgh*, was to be accompanied by new music. Elloran seemed insatiable. He worked as though a demon drove him, almost courting the heresy of utopianism, for he assured by his diplomacy that war would be allayed far longer than the Inquest usually thought suitable. Sajit alone knew what was driving Elloran.

In Varezhdur, the nebula was almost completed.

He and Zhendra made love in a room in the high citadel of Tathenthrang, on a hovercouch that drifted in time to a sad slow consort of hidden shimmerviols. But she was ever more remote now, living in her own imagined world, breathing the dust-made starlight. When they finished he sent the hovercouch flying beyond the balcony, high above the Lake of Octagons. They sat and watched the city, each in his own little silence.

"I hate this city," Zhendra said. "There's no dust here at all. In the morning come servocorpses, scrubbing the stones of the city even where there is nothing left to scrub. It's inhuman."

From the lakeshore to the horizon the terraced levels of the city stretched, each coded in a rainbow color. It was beautiful to Sajit, and tragic too, because Elloran had caused the city to be built in memory of the Rain-bow King, a mad Inquestor who had tried to make a utopia from a dead world, peopling it with corpses that mimicked the living, and festooning the sky with rainbows. It was this utopia that Elloran had undone, so long ago when they had been a soldier-child and an Inquestor-to-be; but it was Sajit who had killed the Rainbow King by breaking his first whisperlyre over his head, to save the boy Inquestor. When the utopia was broken, their friendship too had ended... .

Zhendra said, "That's why I'm a dust sculptress, you know. I see the towers and the monuments, the palaces and the ziggurats, and I see the dust on the streets ... and I know that when the palaces have crumbled the dust will still remain."

She's opening up to me, Sajit thought wonderingly, in the only way she knows how.

"I love you," he said uncertainly.

"Ton Elloran will not let me leave," she said, "after I finish the sculpture. But I must ... I must go to Aëroësh. I must embrace the dust. You must make him ... he has promised to send me, but you know an Inquestor need not answer to a promise... ."

"What influence do *I* have?"

"He trusts you. You did him a lot of good, by bringing him down to the slums of Aírang."

"I turned him into a vindictive monster."

"That too." She looked away. They were circling low over the lake now, sometimes even getting a little wet. Some children in a skiff watched them curiously, voyeuristically perhaps, for Chembrith was a modest world where lovers did not often embrace in the open. Then Zhendra said again, "Aëroësh, Sajitteh. Remember Aëroësh." He could not tell whether she loved him or not. Certainly she had never said so, but he could easily put that down to pride. But she could just be using him as a way to get to the dust world.

"Aëroësh," Sajit repeated listlessly.

The long peace surpassed all their expectations. The Dry Season they spent in Ménjifarn, where the lives of the flora and fauna were counted in minutes and seconds. They watched vast groves of flowers shifting their colors as they died and bloomed afresh, like klomet-wide kaleidoscopes; they watched the birds that soared but once to mate, then plummeted in feather-fluffy rains and cotton-candied into the soft earth. Forests sprang up and toppled, and the only humans were miners who manned the metal mines of the feverlush equator. Varezhdur did not linger, but pinholed further through the overcosm until it reached Gom, where they finished the season with a deep space fireworks of exploding asteroids.

Not nearly soon enough, it seemed to those who attended the Inquestral court, the palace returned to orbit around the planet Alykh, for the Cold Season had begun. Neither Sajit nor the Inquestor would descend to the world below, and so the palace was mostly empty. And Sajit's music remained harsh, and grew ever more shrill and violent as the nebula neared completion. Now they watched her all day, as she worked until she dropped, hardly eating or sleeping. Her cheeks were hollowed out now, her eyes dead; she might have been one of the dying in the Sewer Labyrinth of Aïrang. And the uglier she grew, the more beautiful became the nebula of dust, almost as though she had bequeathed it her own beauty in the final days of breathing life into it.

It was done.

She walked towards the Inquestor on his throne. Sajit saw from the orchestra pit that she could hardly stand. He stopped the music. She whispered "Aëroësh", so softly it could have been a leaf in the wind, and then she stumbled to the displacement plate and dematerialized from the room. Sajit thought she was going to die. He walked up to the Inquestor and looked at him for a long time. His gray eyes were lifeless as polished stone. Half-Alykh filled the blackness beyond the forcedome. Neither of them would look at the dust sculpture. Sajit already knew it by heart anyway. It was about ten meters tall and wide, and it echoed the stars around them, and it drew its stasis-field-power from the starlight itself. Sajit said, "You have to do as she asks, Elloran. You promised, and an Inquestor must always speak the truth."

"Because truth is always defined by what an Inquestor speaks!" Elloran shouted, angry. He drew himself up, shook his shimmercloak straight, and stepped down from the throne. "Are you in love with her?"

Sajit didn't answer. "You're reaching for the impossible, Sajitteh!"

Sajit flinched at the Inquestor's use of his child-name. "She's like me, not like you. She has the Inquestral mind — she sees down to the core of things."

"You are jealous!" Sajit cried out. Then he realized that the musicians were listening. "Neither of us has a hold on her, Elloran. You have to let go."

Then both of them turned to watch the dust as it imitated the stars. But only for a moment. Sajit could not bear it. And Elloran said, "The peace has lasted too long. Next year I will play *makrúgh* for a war."

When she was well again Elloran sent her to Aëroësh, the world at the edge of his kingdom that he had never visited ... she went with nothing but her tools and a little money, taking none of her new fine clothes or the Inquestor's gifts, wearing only the slumsmock she had come in. Sajit watched the tachyon bubble as it passed through the shipwalls to begin its journey through the unseeable tachyon universe.

Then Elloran commanded that the forcedome of the stardust nebula be opaqued and the displacement plates that led to it deactivated. No one would gaze on Zhendra's creation... .

In the throneroom, Sajit relented and played a sweet soothing music, but Elloran asked for the ugly music back. Sajit did as he was told.

Then he went down to Aírang.

Quickly he found the whores' quarter, with its winding alleys flanked by flame-pillars in garish colors, sodium-yellow or copper-blue or potassium-purple, behind which the pimps lurked like cockroaches, avoiding the brilliance of the night sky. He went from pleasure girl to pleasure girl, each one as perfect as the last, devouring them like sherbets. There was no pleasure in the aftertaste. They reminded him of his mother.

When he returned to the palace he found that war had broken out in a distant sector, and Elloran had allied himself with the Inquestor who had styled himself loser. Makrúgh again, played with a vengeance.

Then came a five-year leave of absence, for Sajit needed to be alone, to travel the Dispersal by himself. But he could not forget Dei Zhendra. When he returned it was as though a single breath had passed... .

Varezhdur had grown, of course. The chamber of the dust sculpture was sealed and unreachable; it no longer hugged the skin of the palace and faced the starlight. It was buried under a tangle of gold steeples linked by coils of corridors. Atop the steeples sprouted a bright new amphitheater for grand concerts.

The seasons whirled; there was no news of Zhendra, for the planet Aëroësh could not be reached quickly through the overcosm; a delphinoid shipmind might take subjective years to reach it, and time dilation would take a terrible toll. But Sajit did not want to admit that he had lost her.

One day he was playing a new song in the new amphitheater, scored for a child's voice and a single whisperlyre. The words, in the highspeech, were:

daras sikláh sta lukten z'ombren
af chitaras sereh chom aish
chom daras fah. ...

the stars circle from light to shadow
and even our hearts will become as dust
as the stars have become... .

With an imperious wave Elloran dismissed the orchestra and summoned Sajit to his new throne. The amphitheater was larger than the old throne room, and more austere: no carvings covered the ceilings, no pillars of flame adorned the walls of plain white Ontian marble. Sajit walked the hundred paces from the pit to the throne, a circular reclining throne of white clingfire stuffed with kyllap leaves. He was thinking; Why must he surround himself with such immensity'? Does he want to extinguish himself, like a single dustmote in the emptiness of space?

"My Lord," he said. Elloran struggled to produce

the beginning of a smile; Sajit saw that his eyes had become lined. He had abandoned cosmetic renewal ... he was trying to age, he who had the choice of living far longer than those without power.

"You're still thinking of her!" Elloran laughed drily. "I want to go to Aëroësh, Elloran. I want to see what it is that makes her love the dust."

"There's been no word for years. And if you take a delphinoid ship to Aëroësh there's no guarantee that she won't be dead when you arrive. You know how the pinhole-paths through the overcosm are; space and time lose all meaning, and Aëroësh is too far by objective time for a single lifetime's journey."

"You're toying with me, Inquestor! You know I'm going to ask you for a tachyon bubble."

"Yes, I know." He seemed to sink back even further into the clingfire softness. "Tell me, Sajit ... why is it so important? Why must I kill a star to send you on a mission of unrequited love?"

It was hopeless. "You're an Inquestor," Sajit said bitterly. "You can't possibly understand the love of ordinary people. How can you feel such a thing, you who can pulverize planets with a single word?"

"Sajit, Sajit, I'm not trying to obstruct you, I'm trying to tell you that it's useless...

"Let me see for myself."

"Sajit, you're too proud to see the truth about this love of yours... ."

"You're still competing with me! You with your hundred palaces and your dozen worlds stocked with slaves and your tachyon bubbles and your — "

"I never competed with you. You flatter yourself, that I would condescend to play *makrúgh* with you. Yes, I'll send you to Aëroësh. May the powers of powers protect you."

Sajit closed his eyes then. He wanted to remember Zhendra the way she was when he had first seen her. He knew of the beige hair streaked with turquoise, the eyes like sapphires in cold light, the haunting, taunting voice, the strained remoteness of her when she dreamed up her nebula of dust ... he knew all this but he could not conjure up her image. All he could see was the dust, swirling, whirling, so beautiful you dared not gaze at it for long ... the dust did not swirl for him. It did not need him, or anyone; for in eternity they would all be dust.

"I want a floater to the surface, and a guide."

... a city of drab stone, squat buildings set upon honeycombs hollowed from rock, beneath a forcedome that kept out the sky of red-brown dust... .

"Are you crazy, sir?" The official shivered and offered Sajit a glass of mulled zul. They were in a small evenly lit room of brown rock, reclining on awkward couches of cushioned stone. 'The official was an elder of the city, disturbed and not entirely delighted at the command to entertain a dignitary from. the court that theoretically held sway over the forgotten world. "The dust," he said, "is treacherous. It would kill anyone who went out in it. We do not love the dust here, Shen Sajit. Why, six years ago a woman came, a courtier such as you, sir. She courted the dust — "

"Where is she now?"

The official shrugged. "Your lives are so different, you courtiers. When you are bored of your luxuries you even seek out the deadly, the ugly, the horrifying. I imagine that she sought her own death for some reason that we Aëroëshi are too unsophisticated to understand."

"Was she—"

"Zhonya, Shondra, some name like that... ." He downed his beaker of zul with a single swallow. "In any case, I strongly advise against it. What could possibly be interesting about huge clouds of dust that sweep the plains and would scour and devour everything if there were anything to devour? So what if they sometimes seem to take on lifelike shapes, to mimic starswarms and nebulae as they gust without purpose across the barren lands?"

"They mimic nebulae?" Sajit said faintly. The beaker slipped from his hand. A servocorpse silently removed it and wiped the stain from the polished rock. "Then she's alive! I must go up there now!"

The official laughed. "Give me ten sleeps, maybe more, to find someone foolhardy enough to guide you. It may be that we have a forceglobed flier that can withstand the storms, somewhere in the city. But it will have to be repaired. We have no reason to go out on the surface. We can see the dust from here." And he pointed out of the window, out at the sky.

Sajit trembled, unable to answer.

Erupting from the dust, the floater burst into a scarlet sky. It was an incredibly ancient device built by some hobbyist, perhaps never really meant to fly, that thrust through dust and atmosphere by flinging out a jet of smoke-tinged blue flame. Sajit was not happy with it, even though a darkfield had been added to it and englobed it completely except for the opening for the jetstream. He strapped on his restrainer too tightly and tried to push back as far as he could into the seatcushions. The guide, hardly more than a boy, slipped the vehicle into an airstream and let it coast, raising and lowering its wings according to some mystic-seeming pattern. The flier steadied itself, and Sajit dared to look down.

"I want you to follow the first dust-pattem that you see," he said.

The guide shrugged. He was being well paid, and understood well the idiosyncrasies of the rich. They flew against the sunlight; when Sajit looked through the ring of round windows he saw endless bleakness, brown unbroken flatness. The dust seethed a little, like water beginning to boil, but he saw no works of art... .

"A storm, sir!" the guide shouted. With a wrench he flung the flier into the sun, darkening the field to avoid blindness. Sajit saw nothing —

And then, at the very limits of the horizon, a small smudge shivering like a frightened rodent —

"Follow it!" he whispered urgently. Zhendra must be there. At the heart of the dust. The flier gathered speed, nauseating him.

The dust raced towards them. Without warning they were soaring over it, and Sajit could make out what it was ... the arm of a gigantic spiral galaxy that whirlpooled over a hundred square klomets. His heart almost stopped beating.

"Go into the nebula!" he shouted.

Outside the roar must be like a thunder of lifting starships. Through the portholes nothing could be heard. The dust shifted and sifted like in a dream, too huge to comprehend. She must be in there, he thought. How can I make her understand'? "Can you fly this thing in patterns?" he cried.

"How, sir?"

"The smoke-stream! I want you to bum letters into the dust!"

"I can't go into the nebula, sir! I'm not crazy!" the boy said. 'The flier veered wildly in the wind, losing speed. Soon the dust would swallow it —

"Let's go back!" said the guide.

"Is there a lifecraft aboard this flier?"

The boy nodded. "Take it," Sajit said. "Go back. This thing can't be so rickety that a veteran of the overcosm wars can't at least maneuver it... ." Without a word the boy scurried away. In a moment Sajit saw the small pod thrusting through the dust storm like a lost insect. The boy had not been paid to die, after all. He could not force him... .

The flier spun in the storm, Sajit eased over to the control panel and subvocalized his instructions to the flier's little thinkhive, hoping it was advanced enough to obey him... .

The flier leapt! and swerved! Sickness churned his stomach as the smoke trails formed into zhash, the first letter of Zhendra's name, blue fingers of color against the mud-red —

Again and again, leaping and swerving, the gee-shifts pushing him into his seat and flinging him outward against the restrainers, zhash after zhash in two-klomet-high figures of flame —

He felt the craft weaken against the wind. The voice of the vehicle's thinkhive broke the raging silence:

I am not programmed to deal with such stresses! Please reduce density of programming, pending restoration of flier stability —

Zhash! against the tossing tempest —

Zhash!

Zhash!

The thinkhive's voice — *I am unable to continue with present programming. The craft is now out of control. I cannot hold the forcefield. Environments will interface in a few seconds —*

Sound now, dust hail-pelleting the portholes, whooshing of the storm, ahead, the eye of the nebula unmoving in the turbulence —

I'm going to die.

He was falling. He could not survive. And then there was a frozen moment in which seconds stretched like elastic, and his head was light as though the air were drenched with the drug fang, and the dust was cramming his nostrils but he couldn't feel it —

And then he saw her. The eyes glazed, icy, the

cheeks gaunt, the hair straggly and lustreless, the worksmock torn, the nebula whirling around her, engulfing her and yet coming out of her, just as on the day she had finished the sculpture at Varezhdur —

I'm hallucinating! a small voice inside him whispered.

"Zhendra!" he shrieked, reaching out to embrace the emptiness —

Silence.

***

A chamber walled with dust, sourcelessly lit. Sajit struggled to his feet and looked around him, half-consciously straightening out his kaleidokilt. At first it seemed as though the walls Were motionless; when he stared he saw the chalk-white dust shift almost imperceptibly. The dust was whirling but time itself seemed to have decelerated to a crawl.

And then she materialized. A woman made of dust... .

All dust the hair-strands, dust the eyes, dust the hollow cheeks and sunken limbs, dust the billowing gray smock. Sajit stared at her, not knowing whether to believe his eyes.

"You've become — "

The woman of dust did not speak. She pointed ahead, to the wall: when Sajit turned he saw letters forming out of the dust, words... .

I am the Zhendra you once knew, Shen Sajit of the court of Elloran.

I am the Zhendra you once thought you loved.

"You can't be! I came all this way — "

Don't be unhappy, Sajitteh. Sajit saw the woman smile a little. Specks of dust rained from her lips. *I have found what I wanted. I have found the secret of the dust of Aëroësh... .*

Do you want to know what I know?

The dust has been waiting here for aeons, Sajit. Dust is very patient, you know. There were semi-chains of silicon, almost-

cells of dead stone, waiting for the breath of the ion wind. When the storms came they linked a little, waiting for consciousness. Then I came. I came alone into this wilderness with my little charge-generators and field-generators and my silly little plans for artistic immortality. How stupid I was! The wind tempted me. When I gave myself to it, it was waiting... .

It ate away my body like a fire, Sajitteh. And copied it in silicon. And the dust storm made itself slave to my mind, and it found consciousness ... we are immortal now.

I have given the dust life. I am no longer human, but I am all art, conscious yet created. And I sweep over the dead plains, my body like the galaxy itself, filling the dust with the joy of being alive... .

"Parasites!" Sajit screamed, longing for the woman with the beige hair streaked with turquoise. "They've taken away your soul, everything that made you beautiful... ."

What was there to take, Sajitteh? *I was a nothing woman, a whore among a million whores that garbaged the streets of Aírang. I thought I had a vision — but how can a dead thing have vision? My soul was all I had to give. I dropped it into the dust as a crystal into a saturated solution, and I became one with the dust I loved, I became the soul of the dust ... you should not pity me. You have your music, knit from tragedy and love, and Elloran has his* makrúgh, *but I alone have become a planet's breath, its mind, its life.*

"Didn't you love me at all, then? Did you use us, Elloran and me, merely as stepping stones?" As he said this Sajit realized that this was why he had come. For she had never said that she loved him. He wanted to know which one of the two of them she had favored ... he too had used her. As a way to torture

Elloran whom he envied, as a way to punish himself.

A tear of dust fell from the dust-woman's eye. Her hair seemed to ripple although there was no wind.

Behind her the dust said: *I loved you, Sajit. I loved Elloran. But there are some things greater than love, when you are no longer human ... you could stay here and merge with us, you know. You would know music more perfect than the most accomplished consort of shimmerviols. But I know you will not ... because it is you who do not love me.*

Sajit wept until he was senseless; and the eye of the nebula lifted itself, and the storm shifted until it hovered over the topmost of the tubes that led to the city far beneath the dust, releasing him unconscious; and then the storm fanned out until it made a nebula a thousand klomets wide, larger than a man could ever see except from high up in space ... and the dust danced for itself, heeding no man.

***

The laserdrill shattered the last of the seals and the Inquestor and his musician stepped into the chamber that had lain buried beneath abandoned halls and towers and spiralling corridors, unseen for a dozen years. The darkness was almost palpably intense. Their footsteps rang half-muffled in the hugeness, violating the silence. The air was stale, dusty.

"Thus," said the Inquestor, "we bury our quarrel." He clapped his hands. At once a light-shaft lanced the darkness, a swath of light from floor to ceiling —

The dust, heaped on the mirror metal floor, stirred a little, as the thinkhive that controlled the dust-sculpture searched its memories for the paths that the specks must travel. Silently, the nebula shivered into being out of the cloud, whirling to life. Then the dust danced, always moving yet always one, as the stars have danced since the beginning of time. The arms revolved slowly around a dust-core that blazed in this somber dimness. Fiery dust-specks stippled the imitated sky... . A microcosm dancing with itself. Complete. Alone. Resplendent.

They stood for a moment, too awed for words. Then Sajit said, "I must make a new music to go with this dust. A solemn music, a pavane perhaps." His words pelted the silence. They were unnecessary words. The music, sifting through his mind, said everything.

They walked towards the dust sculpture, two very small people against the vastness.

"I have received a new thought, Sajit," Elloran said. "The thinkhives are buzzing with it. It comes from a far region of the Dispersal of Man, and here the thought is only a faint one, but it is this ... the Inquest falls, Sajit. It will fall soon — in a millennium or less, perhaps. Even though the Fall may never touch us here in our palace of gold."

"It's a terrible thought!" Sajit said, unable to think it clearly.

"No, it's not," said Elloran. Then after a moment he said, "We'll organize an expedition of art-lovers, and we'll go down to Aëroësh and see the dust. She would be pleased, wouldn't she?"

Sajit said — for he had only just returned from the dust-world, and had told Elloran nothing — "How could you have known?" He tried to read the Inquestor's face, tried not to show his own startlement ... but he saw only a cipher. "You knew and you did not warn me?" He felt anger for a moment.

"Could I have stopped you?" And now Ton Elloran had found his throne in the half dark, and he was dusting it with a fold of his shimmercloak. The gesture was a sad one, curiously

touching. "You have forgotten so much, Sajit. You who have known me since I was a child, before I destroyed my first utopia... .
"Do you really think I am not human? Do you really think I can't feel love, pain, the rejection of those I trust, hate, envy? We dare not express these things, we Inquestors, but once I did so, and to a mere soldier-child without a clan... .
"You left my palace when she left, Sajit. You were gone five years. Don't you think I ever longed for her? Don't you think I was ever hurt that both of you had abandoned me? Do you think I never needed to go to Aëroësh for myself, to see for myself, to be convinced for myself that my love was a hopeless one? Sajitteh — "
He stopped for a moment. In the pause, another strain of music coursed through Sajit's mind. "I heard those answers too, Sajit. And at least we have this now. We have both touched the edge of her terrible joy, and it has changed us."
"Elloran— "
"Enough." Elloran's voice had an unwonted tenderness. "At least we will always have this galaxy of dust." He mounted the throne, carefully lifting his shimmercloak for each step of sculpted gold. Then he sat back into its cushions and faced the swirling splendor.

It was then that Sajit understood how deep their loyalty to each other had always been. Even if the Inquest did crumble around them, this loyalty must still stand ... he knew he would always be Elloran's servant, giving music of his own free will, giving love even ... the dust was the great leveller, making the palaces and the slums one.

As always, he waited for a command.

"Go on," said Ton Elloran, "I know you are bursting with music, and you must set it down before it slips away."

Sajit hesitated still. Elloran needed comfort, that was clear. He couldn't bear to leave him alone yet. The stars of dust shone, animated by a woman now transfigured, they shone and shifted and drifted and sifted and made silent music —

"Go!" Elloran whispered harshly. "You are not to see me weep. I am an Inquestor."

Sajit turned his back on the dust-sculpture. The stillness was pregnant, like the hush of a crowd in the seconds before the first note of a new composition. He walked away from the Inquestor's throne, remembering Zhendra's thought:

When we are gone, the dust will still remain.

This story was awarded the Edmond Hamilton Award for "Sense of Wonder" in science fiction, a gorgeous display plaque on a piece of petrified wood.

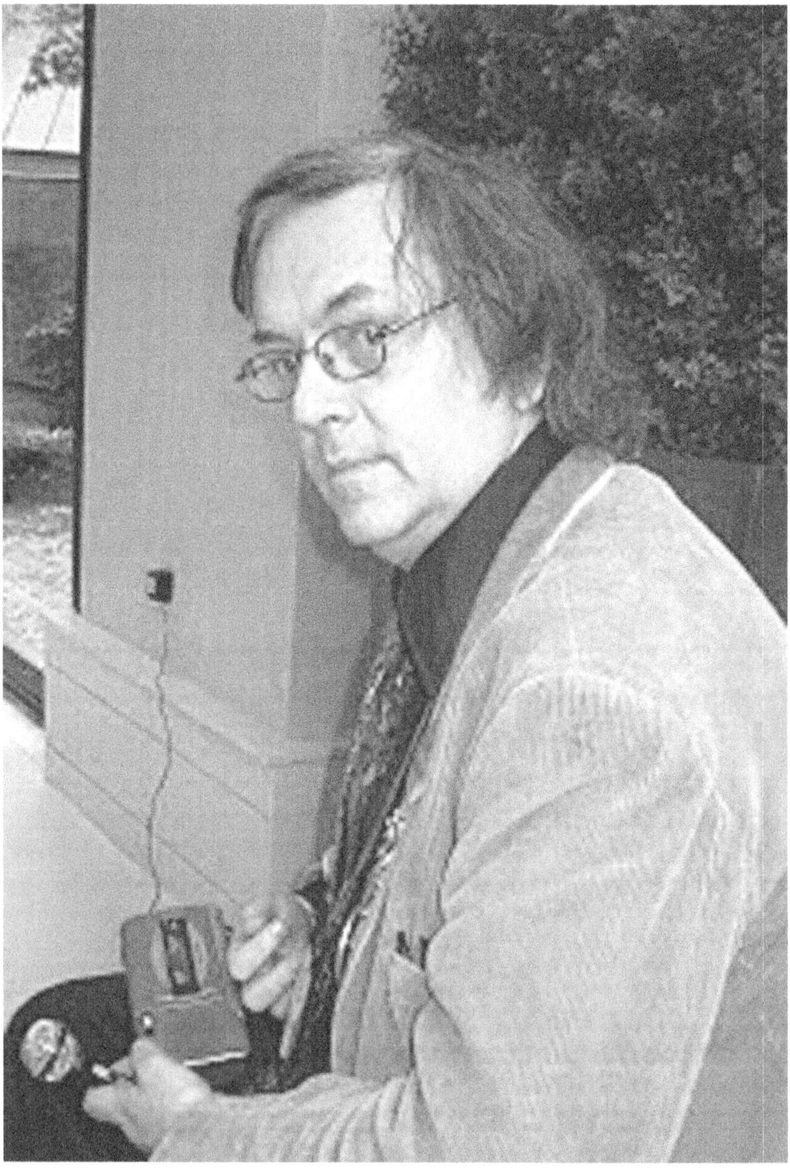

Twenty Years Ago ...

Darrrell Schweitzer talks to Somtow in "ancient times" — an interview from 1998

S.P. Somtow through the curious lens of Darrell Schweitzer

According to Wikipedia, Darrell Schweitzer "is an American writer, editor, and critic in the field of speculative fiction. Much of his focus has been on dark fantasy and horror, although he does also work in science fiction and fantasy. Schweitzer is also a prolific writer of literary criticism and editor of collections of essays on various writers within his preferred genres."

He is two months older than I am, and in certain fields, such as the study of H.P. Lovecraft, he is far beyond me. He's published a lot of books and a whole lot of interviews, and he is one of the science fiction field's genuine eccentrics. He is incredibly smart.

He has interviewed me a number of times, and this is one from about twenty years ago, just before I escaped to Thailand.

S.P. Somtow, whose real name is Somtow Papinian Sucharitkul, is a native of Thailand, who began writing science fiction while living in the Washington D.C. area in the middle 1970's. Some of his science fiction books are *Starship and Haiku, Mallworld,* and the "Inquestor" and "Aquiliad" sequences. He won the John W. Campbell Award for best new writer in 1981. But this was only one of his many careers. He has also been a leading composer of Thai avant-garde music, a musical ghost-writer, a major horror writer (*Vampire Junction* and sequels and *Moon Dance*), and he has directed two films, *The Laughing Dead* and *Ill Met By Moonlight*.

Q: So, you are not merely a well-established fantasy and horror writer, but, I understand, virtually an ancestral figure.

Somtow: Yes, it was Philip Nutman who first said in *The Twilight Zone Magazine* that I was one of the four ancestral figures of the Splatterpunk genre. Frankly, although I didn't know it at the time, I've exploited it. I admit it. I've used "Grandfather of Splatterpunk" on numerous blurbs. It's amazing to me that such a label is necessary, because actually my work hasn't that much in common with Splatterpunk, except of course for large amounts of gore. And even that -- I've mellowed a lot, as far as the large amounts of gore are concerned.

Q: We're talking about *Vampire Junction*, which was a 1984 book. Twelve years ago and you're the *grandfather* of a literary movement that's already passed its peak?

Somtow: Yes, I would consider the entire movement to be dying in its infancy, probably because there is a limit to what one can achieve in such a narrow interpretation of the horror genre. But many of the things that I tried to do in *Vampire Junction*, like writing a novel that's structurally based on MTV videos -- which is really how the novel is put together -- those are things that were new to horror writing and were take up by many people, whether they used that label or not. I think that this is now a common feature of horror writing.

Q: It seems to me that the inherent limitation in the Splatterpunk aesthetic, if we may call it that, is that once you've shown everything, you've *shown everything*, so there is nothing left to show. It's like bringing on the monster in the first reel, so there are no more shocks later on.

Somtow: Yes, that's why I've stopped showing things. I've shift-ed from the showing-everything bit to my mainstream novels, because it's a little more new there. In the book that I'm writing now, *Bluebeard's Castle*, which sounds like a horror novel but isn't, there are a couple of very intense serial-killing scenes that are just passed by in a couple of pages. The whole novel is not like that.

Q: Here again you have encom-passed an entire trend in a couple of pages.

Somtow: [Laughs]. Well, yeah . . . One of the reasons that I had to do that is this is a novel being published in weekly installments, and so one doesnt have more than a couple pages to encapsulate entire trends in.

Q: Are you writing this like a 19th century novel, in that you turn each installment in a week before it appears?

Somtow: No, I fax it in two days before it appears, which gives them no chance to change anything. So I've managed to be really out there, and they haven't been able to do anything about it. So it's very exciting. The first novel I wrote in that way was *Jasmine Nights*, and I found myself becoming more and more daring because of the knowledge that they would print it, no matter how daring I was. So it was a real watershed for me in terms of what I dared to write about.

Q: Where is *Bluebeard's Castle* being serialized?

Somtow: It's being serialized in *The Nation*, an English-language news-paper in Bangkok. Now the English-speaking community in Bangkok is small, but it's frightfully cultural, so I can put in references to really obscure things and it doesn't faze them, which is one of the best things about it.

Q: You could probably slip a horror novel in on them and they'd never know the difference.

Somtow: Well, there are scenes which appear to be horror. The odd thing is that the editor at Hamish Hamilton, who originally bought *Jasmine Nights* after it had been rejected by thirty publishers, had never heard of me, because she didn't read horror or any other genre. She said to me, "I was able to read your novel with an unprejudiced eye because, of course, I don't read genre." Now that the editors at Hamish Hamilton know that I'm a genre writer, they've rejected *Bluebeard's Castle*. They're seeing all these tiny little genre clues in it, which were also present in *Jasmine Nights*, only they didn't know that I was a genre writer. So it's a double-edged sword.

Q: Have you got a publisher yet?

Somtow: Not yet. I'm going to do what my agent did with *Jasmine Nights*, which is what until it's finished. I seem to do a lot better that way, financially at least.

Q: It sounds like a book someone could publish as horror anyway if they wanted to, like that last Tom Tryon novel, which wasn't really a horror novel at all, but was pack-aged as one.

Somtow: It was a Boy Scout Camp coming-of-age horror novel. It *is* horror, but not what you'd think of as horror.

Yes, they may decide that *Bluebeard's Castle* is horror, and if that's the way I have to go in order to pay the mortage, then so be it. But it really isn't.

Q: Apparently horror is absolutely dead as a commercial category right now. So they'll call it "dark suspense" or something like that.

Somtow: The only problem with calling it horror is that this book is hideously funny. All these awful things happen in it, like the heroine has RU-486 administered to her secretly, so her fetus can be aborted and made into a voodoo fetish without her knowledge, and so on and so forth. But she has this cynical sense of humor and is always saying things like, "Yes, it was terrifying, but I was starting to get turned on by it all." This tone is something that might make it a hard sell as a straight horror novel.

Q: Maybe the horror readership is sufficiently jaded that they'll go for it, in the same way that, on one level, Ramsey Campbell's *The Count of Eleven* is a successfully funny serial-killer novel.

Somtow: Yes. That's what I am hoping will happen that people will approach it already jaded, or else it will reach a completely fresh audience that likes to be cynical and likes to satirize itself.

Q: Do you think in terms of being a horror writer or of your work being horror fiction, or do you just let it fly where it may and then let someone else figure this out?

Somtow: I never have thought of myself as a horror writer, and it was only the fact when I did *Vampire Junction* they made me change my name that sort of split me off into a new genre.

Q: Tell the story of why you changed your name.

Somtow: It's a very simple story. Berkley books said that if I changed my name, they'd make me a star. I did and they didn't. But I didn't want to change it too much. It's been a cumulative thing, because, although each edition of *Vampire Junction* has never sold that well, all together it has been quite a large best-seller. It's pretty steady.

Q: I could see it and its sequels as a series of movies. An immortal twelve-year-old vampire rock star has a certain appeal. What a wonderful role for Macaulay Culkin at one point...

Somtow: [Makes sound of distaste.] Mary Lambert, who directed Madonna videos, and then went on to do Stephen King movies, *Pet Sematary* and so on, was very interested in doing the book. We pitched it to Paramount at one point, and the producer there was an ex-starlet. In the middle of the pitching session, she actually asked us if it had vampires in it. So this is about intelligent Hollywood can be at times. She said, "Oh. This book has vampires?" She also asked Mary Lambert who she was. It was very odd. But it seemed to me that someone who had done MTV videos -- she is very famous for doing the Madonna videos, which are very erotic and dark at the same time -- and was able to infuse eroticism into it, would be perfect. She really wanted to do it. She wanted to have Leonardo

DiCaprio play the role of Timmy Valentine -- he's a little old, but it might work quite well.

Q: There may be times when it's more important to get a good actor than to get the age precisely right. It would be very difficult to find a twelve-year-old who could play that part, and if you could get a sixteen-year-old instead, who's good, or somebody who just looks sixteen, then go for it.

Somtow: I agree completely. I've done three *Vampire Junction* books, and I am a little worried that it may be my fate to have to produce another, because sometimes I can go to a publisher and say "I have all these great ideas for books," and I start reeling them off, and they're kind of ho-humming, and then I say, "Then I'll just do you a sequel to *Vampire Junction*." Then they just send a contract. This is frightening to me.

Q: If you're successful enough, you could meet the fate of Edgar Rice Burroughs. You could end up writing twenty-five of them, and readers can predict whole chapters in advance. So I guess you need to reinvent yourself every once in a while.

Somtow: As you know, I really hate to repeat myself that much, and this has gotten me into really bad trouble as a writer. I could have written five hundred *Aquiliad*s or five hundred *Mallworld*s. Or maybe five hundred Inquestor novels. I could have been as big as Stephen R. Donaldson if I'd written five hundred Inquestor novels, for example. Or I could be like Douglas Adams if I had written five hundred Mallworld books. What can I say? I just can't bring myself to do it. There is always a strong temptation to do so, because it's the only way to make money.

Q: Well, you've had your own flirtations with the movie industry.

Somtow: [Laughs.] You could call them flirtations if you like. *The Laughing Dead*, even though it has never been released in this country, has acquired quite a reputation as a cult item, because of the various well-known science fiction writers who appear in it having their heads crushed, and so on. It seems to show up regularly at every science-fiction convention in the video room. In fact it got a rave

review from Michael Weldon of *Psychotronic Film Guide*, which is the imprimatur of greatness among bad horror movies. Then I did the Shakespeare film, because I decided that at that budget I might as well do something relentlessly intellectual instead of just another slasher film, to see what would happen. They didn't go for that either, you know. I made the film and I am still looking for a distributor for it.

Q: You refer to the genre you're working in as "bad horror films," not just horror films.

Somtow: Yes, I have not been working in horror films, *per se*. I have been working in bad horror films, which is a completely different genre from horror films, okay? Bad horror films contain certain elements which are very important. For example, a mysterious villain who speaks in a British accent. There are certain tropes that are required. Therefore, even though my character in *The Laughing Dead* was a Mayan death god, I still had to speak in a British accent because it was a tradition in the bad horror film that this must occur.

Q: Then we're defining the bad horror film as one which is self-aware and campy, with its own aesthetic, like underground art which may be deliberately ugly and crude. All this is different from the merely inept.

Somtow: Absolutely. I am not using "bad horror film" as a perjorative in any way. It is merely a genre with its own tropes, its own sensibilities. I've tried very hard to make my Roger Corman film a bad horror film. But unfortunately it wasn't quite bad enough when it came out, because they had tinkered with the screenplay too much.

Roger asked me to do an adaptation of Bram Stoker's "The Burial of the Rats" as a film, and he just gave me a list of sets that he had acquired the use of in Moscow. They had things like the Bastille, Versailles, these huge historical sets. He said, "Well you can write anything you want as long as it has this title, and I have to have the first draft next week." This was my job interview. "You must use every single one of the sets on this list."

I thought I would create the ultimate bad horror movie in my script, but it didn't work out that way. For one thing, Roger told me that he wanted it to be really wild. But I didn't know that that was a code Roger Corman word for having a lot of tits. I thought he *really* wanted to be really wild. The script is about the young Bram Stoker being abducted in France by lesbian highway-women who are controlled by a mad queen who plays a magic flute and thinks she's Marie Antoinette, played by Andrienne Barbeau. The lesbian highway-women induct him into the ways of feminism, while sitting around being scantily-clad at the same time. We have both left-wing liberal indoctrination and hideous male-chauvinism at the same time, which is kind of cool.

Q: But in a self-aware, parodic way.

Somtow: However, most of the hilarious, pseudo-19th century dialog that I created as been replaced by rather stodgy dialog. Only a few lines, like "I am the Pied Piper's twisted sister" remain.

Q: Do you think you could move into the related genre of good horror films?

Somtow: I don't think I'd want to. I think I'd rather move from bad horror films to a completely different genre, like a mainstream film. Well, that's a silly word too. But the film that I just set up was an art film of the most owing caliber. It a cross between *Sleepless in Seattle* and *The Crying Game*, set in Bangkok.

Unfortunately for me, Margeaux Hemingway was one of the three stars attached to the film, so, because she committed suicide, I was kind of fucked. I'm still hoping to get it back together again somehow. But this was a film that didn't have a taint of horror to it at all, although it does have a shaman who gets possessed by the god Shiva.

Q: There you go. That's enough. But how to you go about getting a film together. A lot of people would like to be movie moguls and make their own films, but you actually got to do it. So what's the difference?

Somtow: The first time, we were subsidized by Lex Nakashima, a well-known science fiction fan. He simply had the money, so that was great. The second time we did it, I sold five-thousand-dollar shares to my relatives and to many other people, who are now breathing down my neck, so I'd better sell the film fast. I got a $100,000 grant from Mr. Sunti who owns *Buzz* magazine in L.A. He's a Thai guy. Because it was culture, Shake-speare and all that, we were able to get a lot of people who wouldn't otherwise do a hideous low-budget film to work for us. Timothy Bottoms, who is definitely an A-list actor, signed up to do it. Other actors, like Robert Zadar, who is only known for being the maniac cop and other monsters in horror movies, wanted to do it so he can say he's done Shakespeare. So we had actors from both sides agreeing to do it.

Q: To get back to horror fiction, we're talking about all these campy, self-aware horror films, but surely you have to control such tendencies in fiction. I don't think there's such a thing as the bad horror novel.

Somtow: Not at all. I think that my horror novels are about as different from my horror film projects as it is possible for two things with the word "horror" in them to be. But there is one thing that they have in common, in a way, is that both the bad horror film and my novels rely a great deal on the hipness of the viewer or reader to catch numerous references. But in my B-movies, those references are to other bad horror films, but in my novels, they're references to works of literature. So it's a different audience.

Q: What do you think makes good horror fiction?

Somtow: I don't know. At first one ought to say that all fiction deals with love and death, and horror, of course, deals with love and death in a very more visceral way. But I haven't been scared by a horror novel in some time, so that's probably not it anymore. If it brings me even a slight flutter of how I felt as a child reading *Some of Your Blood* or something like that, then I feel that I am reading a really good horror novel.

Q: Can you get this feeling while writing something?

Somtow: I aim for that. It's happened only a few times in my writing, when I've actually become absolutely terrified. It's happening less now, I confess. That's why I'm trying to reach out to something even darker, in some ways. I have been doing a series of extremely blasphemous stories lately. I thought maybe that would work.

Q: It would to believers in whatever you're blaspheming.

Somtow: [Laughs] That's true. But even though I am sort of pan-religious these days, I was still brought up in a strict

Buddhist/Anglican environment. Therefore I have two very powerful sets of traditional values working on me.

Q: The readers would be interested, so why don't you say something about your background?

Somtow: When I was six months old, my parents and I left Thailand. My Dad was in the middle of doing his Ph.D. at Oxford, so I grew up in a very dissociative way, because I actually thought I was English. One of my famous statements from my childhood was, "I'm English and you're foreigners," which I said to my parents once. [Laughs.] Then, when I was seven years old, we moved back to Thailand. I spent five years there. I had a tremendous case of culture shock, and I got out of that by retreating into a study of the Greek myths and the classics, and so on. All that is narrated in my semi-auto-biographical novel, *Jasmine Nights*. Everything in the book is sort of true, although not in that order or to that extent. Things like the fellating grandmother who re-moves her false teeth before the act, that, for example, is true.

Q: I know you were educated in Britain, but you have lived in the United States off and on for many years.

Somtow: I grew up in four different countries, but after I started going to school in England, I pretty much stayed there until I was in my twenties. Then I went to Thailand to try to become the Harlan Ellison of avant-garde Thai music. But I got so burned out by that that I came to America and accidentally became a science fiction writer. I actually stayed in America without going anywhere much for about five or six years, but now I have a double life and actually spend a lot of time in Bangkok.

Q: What this must give you is a genuinely unique perspective, by virtue of being an outsider in several cultures at once.

Somtow: Yes, that's right. Wherever I've gone I've always been an alien, which is very frightening, perhaps the most frightening thing about my life. Even when I am with my most intimate family members, I am still culturally a little off from them. I'm the black sheep in both cultures. It's rather scary.

Q: Doesn't this make you observe more, because you take less for granted.

Somtow: Absolutely. I've always said that this is the reason that I've ever acquired skills as a writer at all. I'm spending more time in Thailand, which is really a wild place right now, has caused me to see many more things. As you probably know, Thailand has gone from sort of 1920 to the 21st century in the last ten years. It's amazingly wrenching to see the transformation occur. When I was a child, my house was at the edge of a paddy field, and right now Bangkok is the city with the highest pollution and noise rate in the world, and skyscrapers go up everywhere you look. It's got the world's shopping mall, strangely enough. Not only does this mall have a roller-coaster in it, but there's a little water park where you can get into bumper boats -- on the eighth floor of the shopping mall. It also has the biggest bookstore in the world, by the way. I believe it is like five hundred thousand square feet.

Q: This has also given you a great sense of the absurd.

Somtow: Very much so. Let me give you an example. The last time I was in Thailand, a woman jumped off a building that my family owned in Bangkok. She jumped off and committed suicide, which is very tragic. So then my family had to have the building exorcized. So they sent a fax to the local shaman. That's how things work there. Of course they had to have a religious ceremony right away, to appease the spirit of the woman who had jumped off the building, so it wouldn't jinx the building. But these are people going around in their Armadi suits and acting very modern, and yet they do these things as a matter of course. It wasn't a special deal to them. Of course shamans have beepers and fax machines. There are astrologers in shopping malls.

Q: Just like in the United States.

Somtow: Yes and no. These astrologers actually do your whole chart. They have all the figures in their heads. They're like idiot savants of astrology.

Q: I see how you can get very powerful horror fiction this way, from the fear of never fitting in anywhere. Do you feel this?

Somtow: I do fear it and I live with it every day, so it provides an undercurrent of unease in my life wherever I am, certainly. Do we have enough material now?

Q: Just about. We have a few minutes of tape left, so we might as well use it. I could ask you the meaning of life. Or is that *passé* now?

Somtow: Well, it's not forty-two. In my new book *Riverrun*, I try to answer the question of what is truth, which is pretty deep. The hero is writing an essay about truth. Since it goes through lots of alternate universes, the same essay is shown again and again in terms of the latest universe the characters have fallen into. And the answer he comes up to is that everything is true simultaneously.

Q: I suppose the ultimate question then for the writer is how do you write about truth and horror and your deepest fears without laughing? Is it a good idea not to laugh?

Somtow: I always laugh. As you know, Darrell, I've dealt with some of the most profound questions of life by means of comedy in my works, even in my darkest works. Ed Bryant pointed out that scene in *Vampire Junction* where the kid's entire family has been killed and turned into vampires, and they're sitting around feasting on the blood of a corpse in a video arcade, and they say "You must become one of us now." And the kid realizes that this is the first time he's seen his family have a meal together in years. [Laughs.]

Q: Are there also things which are too uncomfortable to be dealt with in any other way except by laughing?

Somtow: Absolutely. Just because you laugh doesn't mean it's funny. Just because you're terrified doesn't mean it's not funny either. The interface between humor and horror is something that *Bluebeard's Castle* really deals with. So I'm afraid nobody is going to buy it because no one will be able to make up their minds as to whether it's a satire or a novel of suspenseful terror.

Q: It could be both.

Somtow: That's what I'm saying. It is both. But they're going to have to decide what it is before they can sell it. Maybe they'll make a funny cover and a scary cover and have them both out at the same time. That would be good.

Q: One cover could have a laughing face and the other could have embossed entrails.

Somtow: Yeah. I could see that. Or they could do it front and back, and it could be one of those display dumps where the books are facing both ways.

Q: Ultimately everything dissolves down to marketing.

Somtow: I hate to think that, but I've become pretty cynical about marketing. I've decided that I'm just going to write whatever the fuck I want to and let them decide how to package it. I've decided I no longer care, as long as I just get to write what I really want to write.

Q: That's probably a good place to stop. Thank you, Somtow.

Followup 20 years Later:

The novel *Bluebeard's Castle* turned out to be my first experiment in self-publishing, because no one seemed to want it at all — it was too much in between genres. I published it one way, then another, and now it appears as *The Other City of Angels,* from Diplodocus Press.

DESPATCHES FROM EARTH

Butterfly in the Age of Human Trafficking
A production of Madama Butterfly for the 21st Century
reprinted from the Bangkok Post

by S.P. Somtow

This year, I had the chance to direct, conduct and design a production of *Madana Butterfly* all at the same time. This is not because I *wanted* to do all those things — it was because the Bangkok Opera Foundation had no money. The Bangkok Post asked me to write a piece about the forthcoming produciton, so I am sharing it with you now. You can actually watch a rough video of the entire production if you go to vimeo.com and look for "Somtow".

This week, Opera Siam's seventeenth season will close with two performances of one of the "top ten" operas — performed over two thousand times around the world this year alone — *Madama Butterfly*. It's a tearjerker, a relentlessly romantic piece full of famous melodies and a "can't-lose" formula plot: boy meets girl, boy dumps girl, girl kills herself.

When you see this opera on the stages of the world, there's one aspect of the story that doesn't get much play: it's about a rich white man who comes to Asia to exploit an innocent, impoverished underaged girl. At the heart of this icon of romanticism lies a sordid transaction with Goro, called a "marriage broker" — but we would know him as a trafficker.

When *Madama Butterfly* premiered in 1904 it was a total bomb. Some reasons given: people didn't like an opera "set in modern times" — and the hero was just so unlikeable. Well, of course he was. In the original version he had few redeeming features; a racist from the beginning, he never really expresses any remorse at having ruined a young girl's life.

Puccini worked hard to make Pinkerton more user-friendly. In the final version, which is the one we will perform, he makes fewer overtly racist comments and then he adds around 90 seconds of sublimely glorious music in the third act, the aria "Addio fiorito asil" in an all-out effort to show that this heartless baby-stealer has some humanity. Puccini also removed some indications that Butterfly was somewhat more worldly than she is usually portrayed. The "rejected" version was darker than the one we see today, and was a lot more realistic about the "sordid transaction".

The revised edition was a triumph and *Madama Butterfly* is currently the sixth most performed opera in the world.

In our Bangkok production, we are working with one of the most experienced casts ever — both our Butterfly, Nancy Yuen, and our American Consul, Phillip Joll, did their roles in the massively sold-out Albert Hall performances three seasons running, Israel Lozano has sung the role of Pinkerton many, many times. Collectively this cast has done the opera with all sorts of viewpoints and directorial perspectives and in many traditional and non-traditional permutations.

Producing this opera in Thailand, a country in which this plotline happens for real far too frequently, requires that we not ignore the darkness Puccini originally put into his opera. But so often, the music itself, with its vaulting lyricism, its soaring melodic lines, is telling us no: trafficking or trafficking, this is a love that is powerful and real.

If you go back to the original short story and the David Belasco play that Puccini saw and adapted as *Madama Butterfly*, you see a Butterfly much more aware of what is going on, less of a pure innocent. And I think she does know what is going on. Changing her religion is her way of making sure that she doesn't get treated like the other short-time wives she's heard of. I think that at first, this relationship is transactional on both sides. But then, Puccini's music tells us in no uncertain terms that the American predator and the Asian victim arrive at genuine love — that for a short time, that relationship is the real thing. The problem is that, for the man, it doesn't remain real long enough to change him into a different person.

I decided to get at the irony beneath the surface not by disrupting the romantic arc but by finding the ambiguity in the back story. What I'm hoping is that those who come to the production seeking the traditional high romantic rush will get everything they came for, but those who sense an irony in the storyline will see the ambiguity on the edges of the main story.

Some examples: Goro, the wheeler-dealer, has sold Butterfly and the rent-a-wife deal to Pinkerton for "a mere 100 yen", and in the second act he introduces a rich suitor, Yamadori, as everyone assumes that Pinkerton is long gone. In our version we introduce a little backstory; at Butterfly's Act I wedding, Yamadori's already negotiating to be Butterfly's next purchaser. Among the foreign guests at the wedding, the future Kate Pinkerton is already present, and though Pinkerton does not notice her, she's already plotting to get her man one day. The guests at the party, even Butterfly's relatives, all know what the real deal is — this part is explicit in the words that they sing, and most of the time we just see a chorus singing prettily in the background.

So many points of view have been taken with this opera that doing something new just for the sake of it seems pointless. Radical solutions, like having Butterfly pull out a gun and shoot Pinkerton in a sort of turn-the-tables triumph, were proposed, but I've settled for something more understated: as Butterfly goes behind the screen doors to commit suicide, we see, in the distance, her child being delivered to Pinkerton and his new wife — as was the bargain. But Suzuki, Butterfly's maid, appears to tell them something. This prompts Pinkerton to rush to the house, too late to stop the suicide, of course — but now we see him torn between the two worlds; on the one side his romantic love-nest, on the other his new American family, in the distance, with the child that has been purchased at the cost of his mother's life.

Lettercolumn
remarks from our readers...

Write to **inquestortales@bangkokopera.com**

I brought the *Inquestor* novels up from the basement. It has turned into a 5 book trilogy. The back cover of *The Throne of Madness* has melted into the front cover of *The Mind Cage* by A. E. Van Vogt.
— *Fred Cleaver*

As long as there's no e-meter attached.
— *Somtow*

Dear Somtow,

I never read the Inquestor books in the 1980s because I could never find all four books in a bookstore. I read some of the stories in IASFM but never got a complete picture. How can I get a complete set? How many episodes of *Inquestor Tales* will make up the next novel?
— *J.S.H.*

They've now all been made available from Diplodocus Press. If you wait a bit longer, we're doing a new-look 6x9 series with revised text in both hardcover and trade paperback, and improving the kindle editions to be more compatible with different devices, but it will take a while — I am a one-man operation.

— *Somtow*

The Inquestor Series

The Novels

Light on the Sound (1982)
The Throne of Madness (1983)
Utopia Hunters (1984)
The Darkling Wind (1985)

Homeworld of the Heart (in process)
　　Part One: *The Singing Moons* (2018)
　　Part Two: *A Woman Cloaked in Shadow* (2018)
　　Part Three: in process

in process
Vara's World

The Short Stories

The Thirteenth Utopia (Analog, 1979)
The Web Dancer (IASFM, 1979)
Darktouch (IASFM, 1980) (non-canonical)
Light on the Sound (IASFM, 1980)
The Rainbow King (IASFM, 1981)
The Dust (IASFM, 1981)
Remembrances (IASFM, 1982)
Scarlet Snow (IASFM, 1982)
The Comet that Cried for its Mother (Amazing, 1984)

Made in the USA
Coppell, TX
24 November 2024